Misty smiled over at Greg knowingly. "Haven't you ever heard you can't con a con artist?"

She shrugged out of her flight jacket and unzipped her boots. "Hope you don't mind sharing the bed with me. I promise to keep all my clothes on."

Without comment, he turned off the light and stretched out on the bed beside her. She reached out in the dark and slapped his left wrist with the metal object cupped in her hand.

He jerked upright. "What in hell did you just do?"

She lifted her right wrist, displaying the handcuffs stretching between their two hands. "A little insurance to make sure you're still here in the morning."

Outrage lent his voice vibrato. "You *handcuffed* me to you?"

"Clever, aren't I?" she answered perkily. "Sweet dreams, Greg."

Except sleep stubbornly eluded her. The man lying tensely beside her stirred her senses and made her feel nearly as alive as she did when she was flinging a supersonic jet through space. Or when she was getting shot at, she admitted to herself wryly. And that should probably be a warning to her about her misplaced attraction to a defector cum spy.

Dear Reader,

Welcome back to the world of the Medusas! I must confess, I've been especially looking forward to telling Misty's story ever since she sashayed onto my computer screen several years ago.

Can you believe it, but this is the very first time I've written a flying scene in a plane! I tried not to go overboard on the details of flinging a sexy, supersonic jet through the sky, because let me tell you, it's an awesome experience. Please do forgive me if I got a little carried away.

Another reason I'm so excited to share this story with you is that the book's opening scene happened to me in real life. I was near Turkish airspace when it happened, however. The real-life pilot did survive, and he insisted on meeting and thanking me. It was pretty cool. Ever since that incident, I've thought it would make a great book opening. It was a thrill to finally get to write it.

I'm *so* grateful to Silhouette Books for giving my snake ladies an opportunity to continue telling their stories! I have it on good authority that the Medusas are loving their new home at Silhouette Romantic Suspense. So strap on your G-suit, start your engines and enjoy the ride as Misty and Greg hit the afterburners and sweep you away into their Medusa affair.

Warmly,

Cindy Dees

Cindy Dees

THE MEDUSA
AFFAIR

Silhouette®
Romantic
SUSPENSE

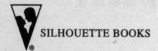

SILHOUETTE BOOKS

ISBN-13: 978-0-373-27547-2
ISBN-10:   0-373-27547-1

THE MEDUSA AFFAIR

Visit Silhouette Books at www.eHarlequin.com

Printed in U.S.A.

CINDY DEES

started flying airplanes while sitting on her dad's lap at the age of three and got a pilot's license before she got a driver's license. At age fifteen she dropped out of high school and left the horse farm in Michigan where she grew up to attend the University of Michigan.

After earning a degree in Russian and East European Studies, she joined the U.S. Air Force and became the youngest female pilot in the history of the Air Force. She flew supersonic jets, VIP airlift and the "C-5" Galaxy, the world's largest airplane. She also worked part-time gathering intelligence. During her military career, she traveled to forty countries on five continents, was detained by the KGB and East German secret police, got shot at, flew in the first Gulf War, met her husband and amassed a lifetime's worth of war stories.

Her hobbies include professional Middle Eastern dancing, Japanese gardening and medieval reenacting. She started writing on a one-dollar bet with her mother and was thrilled to win that bet with the publication of her first book in 2001. She loves to hear from readers and can be contacted at www.cindydees.com.

ting in Russian. She turned up the volume, listening intently.

Good grief.

She transmitted urgently, "Anchorage Center, this is Snake 51. Your unidentified aircraft says he's a military aircraft defecting from Russia. He's been shot. Is requesting clearance to land and an ambulance to meet him. He says he's bleeding badly."

"Roger, Snake 51. Can you relay for me in Russian?"

"Affirmative."

"Tell him we've got him on radar. Ask him what type of aircraft he's flying so I can tell the boys in the bunkers not to shoot him down."

Misty keyed her microphone and said in Russian, "Russian aircraft, I have relayed your message. Say type of aircraft, please."

A pregnant pause stretched out. Finally, the scratchy voice replied, "I am a MiG 55."

Misty's jaw dropped inside her face mask. She'd never heard of such a plane! A new fighter prototype? And it was defecting? Sweet.

Apparently, the air traffic controller needed no translation of that one. He replied, "Snake 51, tell the MiG he's cleared to land at your destination. If you could relay the ILS frequency to him and give him any assistance he needs to set up and fly the approach, that would be appreciated. Tell him an ambulance and fire trucks will be waiting for him at the end of the runway."

The next fifteen minutes were busy ones for Misty, keeping ahead of her own jet and talking the wounded Russian pilot through the Instrument Landing System approach to Camp Green. Worrisome was the way his voice was getting weaker and how he seemed to be struggling to focus on the task of flying his plane. He didn't say any more about his injuries or refer to any further bleeding, but from her first aid training, he sounded on the verge of passing out.

She transmitted, "Still there, Russian jet?"

"Yes," he replied grimly.

"Stay with me. You're almost there. Do you have the field in sight?"

"Not yet."

"What's your altitude and airspeed?"

He relayed the numbers to her, albeit sluggishly. It sounded as if he was fighting for all he was worth to stay conscious and concentrate on flying.

"Is your gear down and locked?"

"Yes."

"How about your flaps? Are they configured for landing?"

"Yes."

"Are you on glide slope?"

"Uhh, I'm high."

"Power back a little and push your nose down."

"I know how to fly," came the snapped response.

Excellent. That sounded a little more alert. "Let me know when you've stabilized on course and on glide slope."

"I will." For a moment his voice took on a mellow resonance. "And in case I don't make it, thank you for your help."

A chill raced down her spine. He *had* to live! "We've come this far together, MiG. You'll make it. I promise."

"You have a beautiful voice. I imagine you are as lovely as you sound."

"Let me know after we both land. How's that approach looking?"

The radio went silent while the Russian established himself on the narrow beam radio signal that extended up and out from the end of the runway, which a plane could follow right down to the first brick of the runway.

Misty checked her own fuel gauges, which were getting alarmingly low. She'd been orbiting high over the field for the past fifteen minutes to conserve fuel and concentrate on talking to the Russian. If he crashed and closed the runway, she was going to be in a world of hurt. She had barely enough fuel to make it through her own approach, let alone fly to an alternative airfield after this unscheduled loiter.

"How're you doing, Russian aircraft?"

"I see the field."

"Do you want to transition to a visual approach or continue the ILS?"

"I better stay on instruments. My eyesight's going."

Not good. One of the last functions to fail before losing consciousness was the eyes. Pilots called it graying out. Everything they saw became a gray blur. The guy was putting up a good fight to make it to the ground, though. Tough customer. Brave. Maybe a little crazy, too, to have stolen a MiG prototype and raced it across the Bering Strait.

"Hang in, MiG. You're almost there."

"Roger," he ground out.

"Keep talking to me," she urged. "How far out are you now?"

"Six…miles."

A hundred and fifty knots, which was a typical fighter jet approach speed, was roughly two-and-a-half miles a minute. A little over two minutes until he'd be on the ground.

The air traffic controller broke in, transmitting urgently, "He's getting low. Tell him to pull up!"

Damn. Her brave MiG pilot was losing it. "Pull your nose up," she translated sharply. "Pay attention! You made it all the way from Russia. Don't blow it now. You owe me a drink after this!"

To the air traffic controller she asked in English, "How's he doing?"

"Better. Coming up to glide slope."

In Russian, "How far now, MiG?"

"Three miles."

"Heck, you can glide in from there. No problem," Misty teased gently, "A lot of folks are watching you. Make it a pretty landing."

The Russian grunted back by way of reply. *C'mon, you can do it!* She forced her white-knuckled grip to relax on her own control stick. He'd gone too silent. She tipped up on her left side momentarily to peek below. His jet was medium-gray. And it was drifting well right of the runway centerline. *No!* He couldn't lose it now! He was so close!

"Fight, dammit! Stay with me! Fade left and get yourself back on centerline!"

"For you...I will try."

She watched the clock tick in her own cockpit, the second hand sweeping slowly around its face. And then there was one last transmission, barely audible, from the Russian. "I'm on...the ground." A long pause. "Thank you."

She sagged in relief. But she couldn't let down for long. She had her own approach to set up and fly. She dropped the flaps and gear, ran a before-landing check-list, and intercepted the ILS. A vehicle with red flashing lights raced away from the far end of the runway toward the low cluster of buildings that made up Camp Green. An ambulance. The Russian pilot must still be alive, then. Thank God.

She made out the sleek, muscular shape of his jet on the taxiway, but couldn't see any details from this distance. She'd love to get a better look at that prototype later. And then the ground came rushing up at her, the grass whizzing by at 160 knots, demanding her full attention. She pulled on the stick until the jet's rear wheels kissed the runway with a gentle squeak. She set the nose down smoothly, applied the brakes and taxied to parking.

She popped open her canopy and a pair of crew chiefs ran up to the T-38 and hung ladders on the front and back cockpits. She finished buttoning down the plane and climbed out. A signature in the maintenance log, and she was free to go.

General Wittenauer fell in beside her as they headed for base operations. "Just another day at the office, eh?" he commented.

She smiled over at him. "After you've been shot at enough times, things like that aren't even exciting any more." She was lying of course, all in the name of being cool. That guy had gotten to her. Something about his voice connected with her…and she was waxing hokey in the extreme. He was just some Russian pilot who'd defected.

Beside her, the general said, "Becoming jaded is the price you pay for playing with the big boys."

"I'm not complaining. I love my job."

Who wouldn't? Getting to be on the first all-female Special Forces team in the U.S. military? It rocked, being one of the Medusas. Right now the team was on a break, standing down after several months of continuous missions. The other women were basking on beaches in various parts of the world, healing from their injuries and getting warm after their arctic training in northern Norway last month.

Well, it had started out as training at any rate. The junket to Norway had turned into a full-blown mission before all was said and done, with her boss, Vanessa Blake, and team member, Aleesha Gautier, both getting shot, and Karen Turner nearly dying from ingesting a lethal chemical.

While the rest of the Medusas worked on their tans, her idea of a vacation was to get back into the air. The team's only pilot, she'd used the break to renew her flight currency and log a few hours. Another perk of being a Medusa. Vance Air Force Base in Enid, Oklahoma, had made a T-38 and a fuel credit card available to her for as long as she wanted them.

As she walked toward base ops, the adrenaline surge of talking down the Russian pilot finally drained away, leaving her abruptly fatigued. Inside, a sergeant took her parachute, g-suit, and helmet from her to inspect and store. Two army officers met General Wittenauer and herded him off toward his briefing. She headed over to the dormitory shared by everyone stationed at the camp. It was easy to spot—it was the only two-story building on the whole base.

She collected a room key and let herself into a sparsely furnished room. Linoleum floor, steel bed, three-drawer chest, a table and chair, television. Funny how her standards in quarters had changed. Time was when she wouldn't have considered staying at anything less than a world-class, five-star hotel. Nowadays, it was pure luxury simply to have a roof over her head and sheets to sleep on. And she wouldn't trade the satisfaction of this job for anything in the world.

She pulled off her flight boots, slid the wooden blackout panels across the window, and fell into bed.

Yep, just another day at the office.

In a surprisingly civilized corner office on the top floor of the Lubyanka—a former KGB prison in the heart of Moscow—General Karkarov looked up. His personal assistant, a former KGB man himself, stepped inside and closed the door.

"The plane made it to Alaska, General."

"Did the pilot live?"

"Apparently. An ambulance was seen taking him to a medical facility."

Karkarov swore loud and long. "Pursuit planes were not able to catch the MiG?"

"The local air defense forces were caught napping. The MiG had about a ten-minute head start by the time anyone could even consider giving chase. There was no way to catch the jet before it entered U.S. airspace."

Karkarov nodded grimly. "You know what to do, Gennady. The Americans must not get a good look at that plane."

Misty jerked awake some time later. No light seeped through the cracks in the shutters. Dark outside, then. What woke her up?

Someone knocked on her door again.

She skated across the slippery linoleum in her socks and opened the door. A man she'd never seen before stood there, wearing khaki slacks and a navy-blue sweater with no rank on it. A civilian? Up here? This was a highly classified *military* Special Forces facility.

"Captain Cordell?"

"Yes."

"I'm sorry to bother you in crew rest, but we need to talk to you."

"We who?"

"CIA."

She noted he didn't volunteer a name. "I didn't know you gentlemen were up here. Just a moment while I get my boots on." She stepped into her flight boots and zipped them up quickly. "How cold is it outside?"

"'Bout freezing."

Not bad for April in Alaska. She grabbed her flight jacket and followed the silent CIA agent across the compact compound to a long, low building—combined infirmary and communications facility.

"This way," he said, opening a door for her.

She stepped into a generic briefing room. Long table, a dozen chairs, whiteboard on one wall. Another civilian waited at one end of the table. Like the first man, he was of medium height, medium build and medium coloring. He, too, didn't introduce himself to her. Must be covert operators. Desk-jockey analyst types usually didn't care if you knew their names.

She closed the door. "Let me guess. Agent Smith and Agent Jones."

The men gave small smiles. "Close enough," the one she'd dubbed Jones replied.

"What can I do for you gentlemen?"

Jones answered, "As you know, a prototype Russian military aircraft landed here today."

She nodded.

"Its existence needs to remain secret for obvious reasons. It has been classified Top Secret, and we'll need you to sign a statement to that effect."

"Fine. But surely you didn't interrupt my crew rest just for that."

"No. There's more." The two men exchanged glances, and Jones spoke again. "It's about the pilot you helped."

"The Russian? How's he doing?" she asked in quick alarm.

"He'll live. A bullet lodged in the meaty part of his left thigh, but it was removed and the bleeding stopped. He's asking to speak to you. Wants to thank you in person for helping him land safely."

Anticipation leaped in her throat. She wanted to meet him, too. Something had happened between them up there in the sky. Some sort of…pull. "Let's go see him."

"Not so fast."

Misty frowned.

"You need a little background information before you meet him. The pilot's name is Vasily Nemorov. We don't know a whole lot about him."

She replied, "Well, you know he's probably a Russian military test pilot since he had access to a MiG 55. And he doesn't speak English—or at least not when he's under extreme duress."

The two men exchanged cryptic glances, and Jones continued. "He's refusing to tell us anything more than his name, rank and serial number."

"He's had a shock. Probably had the heck brainwashed out of him about you CIA types, too."

Both men frowned. Jones said grimly, "You have no idea how accurate your observation might be. We don't know exactly how big a shock he's had nor how brainwashed he is."

Concern flooded her. "Is he seriously injured?"

"Not particularly. He only had that one wound. Mostly he just lost blood. They put three pints back in him."

"But he's going to be all right?"

"Oh, yes. He'll be fine physically. But here's the thing. He's not a pilot. And he's not Russian."

She absorbed that punch in the gut for a moment. "I beg your pardon?"

The CIA agent's voice dropped to bare murmur. "You heard me."

"How do you know he's not a Russian pilot?"

"Because he's not Vasily Nemorov."

"Then who is he?"

Another pregnant look between the two men. They both sighed heavily. Then Jones said, "We need your help, Captain Cordell. We need you to talk to him. Establish trust with him. Communicate with him."

"To what end?"

"To find out what in the bloody hell he's up to!" Smith blurted.

She was missing something here. How could he not be a Russian pilot? How else would he have gotten access to and flown out a secret MiG prototype? It made no sense. "Who *is* he?"

Jones picked up the conversation again. "His name is Greg Mitchell. He's an American. A spy. He works for us."

American? A CIA agent? "How come he doesn't speak English? Is he a Russian native you guys turned?" Although a name like Greg Mitchell certainly *sounded* American.

"No. He's from California. Los Angeles."

"Okay. I'm confused. What's going on here?"

Jones huffed, obviously frustrated. "That's what we're hoping you can find out. This guy is definitely Greg Mitchell. We have fingerprint and DNA matches identifying him as the guy lying in the room down the hall. Yet he appears to speak no English nor have any recollection of being an American citizen. He was sent into Russia nearly five years ago, on a quick in-and-out mission to deliver a Russian spy back into the custody of the Russian government. A no-brainer. Except the hand-off went bad. Someone started shooting and the Russian was killed. And Mitchell disappeared. Completely. The agency wrote him off for dead. Now, all of a sudden, he comes streaking over the horizon in a jet no one's ever heard of."

"Does he have amnesia?"

"He shows no indication of it."

"Drugs?" she suggested.

"The docs find no evidence of that either, although they don't have the highest-tech gear available up here. They've sent blood and tissue samples out for analysis."

Smith added, "For whatever reason, he seems interested in talking to you, Captain. Perhaps because you saved his life, perhaps because you're a woman. Hell, maybe because you have a sexy radio voice."

Misty's jaw tightened fractionally. They all did that. Men took one look at her and saw a Barbie doll good for only one thing.

Unaware of his blunder, Smith continued, "We're hoping he'll talk more freely to you than to us. After all, you're beautiful and charming."

Right. At least he'd gotten far enough past her looks to add charming to her list of attributes. Maybe he'd suggest that she'd make a lovely hostess next. After all, she could put on a tea party or fancy soirée with the best of San Francisco high society.

"We need some answers. We need you to find out what happened to him. Why is he no longer Greg Mitchell?"

Chapter 2

Misty paused, her hand on the door handle, and collected herself for a moment. She consciously set aside her irritation at the men who'd sent her here, focusing instead on the bond she already felt with the man on the other side of the door and her intuition that he needed her help.

She stepped inside the simple hospital room, her orders firmly in mind. Of course, the unspoken, and possibly most important, order hanging in the air was to find out what had happened to Mitchell's original mission in Russia.

A dark-haired man lay in the room's lone bed, gazing out the window. His head turned quickly at the sound of her entrance, the expression on his face cautious. *Wow*. To say he was good-looking didn't begin to do this man justice. Various descriptions floated through her head, disjointed. Dashing. Aristocratic. Cary Grant suave.

"*Zdrastvuityeh.*" Hello.

"How are you doing?" she replied in Russian.

He replied in the same language, a sexy murmur that shot across her skin like the clean, fiery bite of vodka, "Ahh, my American angel. I would know your voice anywhere. You are even more beautiful than I imagined." He struggled to sit up straighter and a wince crossed his features.

She pulled up the room's only stool and perched on it beside the high bed. A hint of a smile crossed his face, and it was the most natural thing in the world to smile back. She was not the kind of woman to go all trembly inside over a smile from a good-looking man, but her innards abruptly felt, well, trembly.

"Captain Cordell," he murmured.

"How—" And then she remembered. She was still wearing her flight suit, and it had a nametag in addition to the captain's bars sewn on its shoulders. "They told me your name is Vasily." Better stick with his Russian persona for now.

He shrugged noncommittally.

"How are you feeling? Are they taking proper care of your injuries?"

That earned a smile out of him. And another zing of attraction straight to her core. He had perfectly straight teeth—a dead giveaway that he'd spent his childhood in America. But more to the point, he had dimples. Sexy, boyish ones that practically curled her toes. His sable eyes were extraordinary. The intelligence shining in them was palpable. She got the distinct feeling those eyes didn't miss a thing that went on around them.

"I will make a full recovery. Thanks to you. I have no words to express my gratitude for your help today."

"My pleasure. I'm just glad I was in the air and on the radio at the right time."

"It was fate," he murmured.

A chill shivered down her spine. *Fate indeed.* "Can you tell me anything about how you got out of Russia?"

He flashed her those devastating dimples again. "I turned east, pushed the throttles forward as far as they'd go, and flew until people threatened to shoot me down."

She smiled, concealing her thoughts. *Going to be evasive with me, is he?* Just as well. She wasn't thrilled at the idea of pumping this man for information, not so soon after his ordeal and particularly not by taking advantage of the bond they'd formed up there in the sky. She glanced down at the heavy bandage swathing his thigh below a pair of gym shorts. "How's your leg?"

"Better. They gave me blood. I'm three pints American now."

"Not to worry. You'll just have inexplicable cravings for junk food."

He laughed aloud, a warm, masculine sound.

"As a fellow pilot, I have to ask. What can you tell me about your MiG?"

"You can see it from the window," he replied cautiously.

"Really?" She got up and moved over to the window. A sleek, space-age-looking silhouette was indeed visible on the ramp beneath a netting of camouflage fabric. Based on its shape, it obviously incorporated radar invisibility technology.

"Good-looking jet. Nice lines."

He spoke from the bed. "She's nearly as elegant as you."

Misty didn't know what to say. Men hit on her all the

time, to the extent that she generally considered herself immune to come-ons. But she was rarely compared to a supersonic jet, and the murmured compliment touched her aviator's soul. It did not, of course, have anything to do with the man delivering said compliment. No, sirree.

She turned to thank him, but the door opened just then. A male nurse walked in. His eyes opened in brief surprise when he spied Misty, but then he continued forward toward the bed.

In English, the nurse said, "It's time for your shot, sir." He held up a syringe and showed it to the Russian.

Misty translated quickly.

"No shots," Greg replied to her in short, sharp Russian.

The nurse didn't wait for her to translate. He explained, "But he needs this. It's an antibiotic to prevent infection."

Misty translated again.

The Russian pilot pasted on a fake smile aimed at her and muttered from behind it, "They already gave me anti-biotics and said I wouldn't need more tonight."

Their gazes connected. The simpatico they'd forged in the air roared to the fore, and shared suspicion flowed between them. Something was wrong with this 'nurse.' They both sensed the threat.

She continued to smile pleasantly back at him and murmured from behind her own plastic smile, *"Ponyat-nuh."* Understood. And she did. With crystal clarity. He also thought this guy wasn't a nurse and that wasn't peni-cillin in the syringe. It made sense that the Russians would want a defector dead. But to have found him so fast? Was a sleeper agent already in place at Camp Green? How was that possible?

She stepped closer to the bed, reaching out to rest a hand on Vasily-Greg's shoulder. A simple, comforting gesture. But surreptitiously, her fingers gripped his T-shirt tightly. "Ready to roll?" she murmured in Russian. The double entendre was the same in both languages.

"Mm-hm," he murmured.

"I'm afraid there's been a mistake," she said smoothly in English to the 'nurse.' "He says he already had his injections for the night."

"Oh. It wasn't recorded properly in his chart then." The nurse spoke easily, but Misty noted the shift of the needle to his left hand and the casual drop of his right hand to the pocket of his lab coat. The pilot's shoulder went tense beneath her hand. He'd seen the move, too.

The nurse's hand came out of his pocket in a blur, but Misty was ready for it. She yanked Vasily's T-shirt with all her might at the same time he flung himself toward her. The combination rolled him out of bed and into Misty's body milliseconds before the feather pillow in his bed exploded to the spitting sound of silenced bullets.

Misty crashed to the floor with Vasily on top of her. He continued his roll and was off her before his weight had barely landed on her. She dived underneath the bed, which blessedly was an old-fashioned affair with lots of open space beneath it. A pair of bullets spat overhead and glass shattered behind her. So much for the window. She lunged for the shooter's ankles, wrapping her arms around them and yanking them out from under the guy. The assailant crashed to the floor. She scrambled forward, grabbing for his gun wrist. Another bullet winged into the ceiling as they struggled.

She sprawled on top of him while he tried to force her to one side. He braced his legs wide and shoved up and over—a classic wrestling move. Quickly, she shifted her hips so her legs fell between his and jerked her knee up.

Hard. Between his legs. *Not* a classic wrestling move. The strength abruptly went out of the man's gun hand and he yelled out a curse.

She wrenched at the gun as the guy tried to twist it out of her grasp. It went off again, sending a bullet through the guy's cheek. He stared at her in surprise above his ruined face for several seconds, and then his eyes rolled up into his head. She felt for a pulse in his throat. Nothing. Lucky shot. Must have penetrated through the mid-brain and scrambled his brain stem where vital life functions originated to have killed him so quickly. She closed her eyes for a moment, willing away the shakes.

She gathered herself quickly and rolled off the dead man, taking his pistol with her. Crouching, she ran over to the closed door. Pressed her ear to it for a second. Silence. She stood to one side and yanked it open. Nobody burst in. She spun out into the hall, the pistol chest-high in both hands. Clear right. She spun left. An orderly who was walking down the hall toward her started violently and dived for the floor.

"Get some help! A man's been shot in here!" she called.

She raced back into the hospital room. A quick glance around. Where was Vasily-Greg? Cold air blew in through the gaping window. She ran over to it and looked out into the night. No sign of him. He was out there somewhere, possibly hurt and definitely severely underdressed for the elements.

She cursed under her breath, grabbed her flight jacket, and vaulted out the window behind him. Voices shouted behind her as she ran away from the hospital. She'd explain to the authorities later. Right now, she had to find the missing pilot!

For no other reason except instinct, she headed for the

MiG. It was the one familiar thing to him in this foreign place, and it already represented escape to him. It stood nearly a mile away at the end of the runway under its camouflage drape.

The good news was that she was a triathlete in her free time and her work in the Medusas also kept her insanely fit. The bad news was that, even with a leg injury, her quarry had a good head start on her. She was about halfway to the MiG when she thought she spotted a dark shape hop-skipping ahead of her toward the jet.

She put on an extra burst of speed, calling out low in Russian, "It's me, Vasily. Your attacker is dead."

No response. *Damn.* She'd lost sight of him again. She continued forward, searching the night for her man.

Without warning, a streak of brilliant light flashed down out of the heavens in front of her. It fell at hypersonic speed, like a meteor headed straight at her. She stopped in her tracks, staring up at fiery death. A spectacular flash blinded her as the flaming object slammed into the MiG. The explosion of light and deafening concussion of sound struck her simultaneously, knocking her backward and flattening her on the ground.

Holy Mother of God. A missile had just destroyed the MiG!

She blinked fast, but the painfully white afterimage in her eyes wouldn't go away, nor would the high-pitched ringing in her ears. She stuck her fingers in both ears and pulled them out, inspecting her fingertips for blood. Shockingly, there was none. She'd have laid odds the explosion had burst her eardrums.

She pushed up to her feet, looking around for Vasily-Greg, the night now brightly illuminated by burning wreckage. Sirens wailed, piercing her temporary deafness, and people were running this way. Small brush fires burned all around the MiG, or at least the crater where the MiG used to be. And debris was still raining down out of the sky, falling to the earth with metallic thuds. Despite the danger, she ran toward where she'd last seen the missing pilot.

"Vasily!" she shouted into the cacophony of secondary explosions, sirens and screaming voices.

Close enough to the remains of the MiG to feel the heat of the fire consuming it, she stumbled onto the prone body of a man. *Oh, God.* She dropped to her knees beside him. Was it the Russian? Was he dead? She rolled him over gently.

Not him. *Thank God.* Based on this man's camo clothing and the rifle still clutched across his chest, he must be one of the guards who'd been walking patrol around the MiG. He was alive, but unconscious. She checked his vitals quickly—pulse steady, airways clear, breathing regular, no excessive blood loss.

She stood up, waving her arms over her head and shouting to draw the attention of the firefighters just arriving on scene in their truck. Several firefighters ran across the grass toward her. She turned the guard over into their care and moved on, searching the faces starting to gather for any sign of her handsome quarry. He had to be here somewhere. After all, he'd been closer to the MiG than she when the missile hit it.

Nothing. Not a trace of him. She swore under her breath as she looked around. What a mess. Fragments of the jet lay all over the place. Gradually, her eyesight returned to normal and the ringing in her ears subsided to a mildly irritating squeal. Firefighters sprayed water on the flaming wreckage, and the glow around her dimmed. Where the hell was he?

She stumbled over a piece of debris and glanced down, startled. It was a charred, blackened, but intact, metal box, about eighteen inches by eighteen inches and about eight inches thick. It looked like a computer. She squatted down to examine it more closely. It didn't have slots for computer disks or ports to plug in accessories, just a few bundles of wire sticking out of one side. In fact, now that she looked at it more closely, it could be a black box. Was this the MiG's vitally important Flight Data and Cockpit Voice Recorder? Investigators might not have the jet itself any more, but if she was right, they'd have a whole bunch of data about what the MiG could really do.

She carefully lifted the box in her arms. It was heavy— thirty pounds or so—probably due to the metal tape used to inscribe the plane's flight data and radio transmissions as indestructibly as possible. A cluster of men stood beside a fire truck, waving their arms and talking on radios as though they were attempting to supervise this chaotic scene. She was heading for them when the sound of an engine roared up behind her. She glanced over her shoulder and made out a military police jeep bumping toward her over the grass. It pulled up beside her and the passenger door opened.

An urgent voice said in Russian, "Get in."

Vasily-Greg! *Thank God.* Running away was he? Not that she could blame him after that "nurse" had tried to kill him. Smith and Jones would have a cow if the Russian pilot escaped. Should she try to talk him out of leaving? But then she spied the grim set of his jaw, the determined glint in his eyes. Nope. He was leaving. Tonight. She dared not let him waltz out of here alone like this. If this guy was brainwashed or amnesiac, someone needed to keep an eye on him. Not to mention, nobody knew what he was really up to. Was he a simple defector, or was there more to him?

"Hurry!"

She climbed into the vehicle, cradling the electronic piece in her lap. The jeep roared off into the unknown.

A cascade of relief flooded Vasily as the American pilot climbed into the jeep beside him. He didn't stop to examine its cause too closely. Perhaps it was because she was his only ally in this dangerous sea of strangers. Or perhaps it was because she'd already saved his life twice that he trusted her not to harm him. Or perhaps it was because he'd been so mesmerized by her beauty when she'd stepped into his hospital room and smiled at him that he'd thought for a moment he'd died and gone to heaven.

"Are you all right?" she asked.

He shook himself out of his musings and paid attention to where he was going. They had to get out of here. Fast. Before some other Russian double agent tried to kill him. "I'm fine. You?"

"Me, too."

He let go of the steering wheel with his right hand and reached over to place a hand on her shoulder. "Thank you for saving my life—again."

Her shoulder was slender, feminine even, but he felt the strength of the muscles beneath his fingers. An interesting contrast. Warmth spread outward from his fingers. And then the jeep hit a bump and he had to grab the steering wheel with both hands. But his fascination with his impromptu companion continued to multiply.

She cleared her throat, sounding uncomfortable. "Good timing on your arrival. This thing is heavy. I'm headed for those men over there." She pointed through the windshield.

He nodded and guided the jeep around part of a wing lying mangled on the ground. He veered further to the left around more wreckage. And then he bumped out onto the runway and accelerated—away from the men she wanted to give the box to. Nobody was getting their hands on that box in her lap until he was finished with it! It was the whole reason he'd fled Russia, after all. What a piece of luck that Misty had found it for him.

"Hey! What are you doing?" she squawked.

He glanced over at her grimly. "I have to get out of here. People are trying to kill me."

"Vasily, this entire camp is crawling with Special Forces soldiers. You couldn't be in a safer place, shy of locking yourself in an underground bunker."

"Do you know where one is?" he retorted.

"I'm serious. You're safe here."

"Right. And that's why a man came into my room with a needle full of poison and a gun in his pocket."

"Okay, I'll grant you that. We obviously had a sleeper agent in our midst. Although how in the world that happened, I can't fathom. Nobody ought to be able to slip past the background checks Special Forces types have to go through."

He threw her a sardonic look. "Your government has contracted out security checks for the past decade. How did one of your astronauts put it? It's not a comforting thought to be orbiting in space in a machine built entirely by the lowest bidders?"

"True." She sighed.

A pang shot through his gut. He was incredibly adept at distracting people from the point of a conversation. But he hated using such tactics on her. She'd been nothing but kind to him so far. A terrible thought slammed into him like a bucket of ice water. What if she was playing on his trust? Manipulating him to find out what he was up to? God, he got sick of the mind games that came with his profession.

"Where are we going?" she asked.

As much as it pained him to answer her question this way, he said firmly, "*We* are not going anywhere. I am leaving the base with that box and you are getting out of the jeep as soon as I'm safely away from the security perimeter."

"Do you think it's a good idea to ditch me so quickly?" she asked reasonably. "I'm American. I know this area. I speak the language. Don't you think a Russian man driving around in a stolen military jeep, wearing shorts and a torn T-shirt, is going to be a little bit too visible?"

If he were, indeed, a Russian pilot, her argument would make perfect sense. He'd be nuts to turn down her offer. He replied cautiously, "How do I know you are not one of them? While I am grateful for your help, I cannot let a potential CIA agent ride along with me as I attempt to escape that very agency."

"I'm so *not* a CIA agent." She laughed.

He cocked a skeptical brow at her, then returned his gaze to the dirt road as a guard shack came into view.

"Let me do the talking," she ordered quickly. She wrestled the blackened box down to the floor at her feet, then shrugged out of her jacket and threw it over his legs.

The guard on duty waved the jeep to a stop.

As he slowed, Misty murmured, "Roll down the window." And then she all but lay across his lap to peer out at the guard. *Hello, beautiful.*

She called out cheerfully, "Hi, Randy. How'd you get stuck out here, missing all the excitement over at the airstrip?"

"Just my lucky day," the big man answered gruffly.

"FYI, the sky cop pulling guard duty around the plane that blew up is gonna be okay. Doesn't look like anyone was killed in the explosion."

"Do they know what happened yet?"

"Nah. It'll take the investigators a while. Heck, for all I know the Russians had some sort of self-destruct mechanism built into the MiG."

Vasily snorted mentally. The Russians were paranoid, but they didn't think that far ahead. They weren't as good as they used to be in the good old days of the Soviet Union.

The guard asked casually, "Where ya headed tonight?"

The lovely American answered equally casually, "An after-dinner meeting. Off base, with some congressional staffers. We don't want them crawling all over this place if we can avoid it."

She really was very good. There wasn't a hint of tension or stress in her voice. This American pilot had strong nerves.

The guard snorted. "No kidding. Not unless they've come prepared to hand out a lot of money."

"We'll see. That's what General Wittenauer's hoping for."

The guard nodded and stepped back. "Y'all have a nice night." He saluted smartly, and Captain Cordell returned the snappy gesture.

Greg drove the car through the gate. The one-lane track only headed in one direction. He followed it into the darkness for a long while in silence.

Finally, he muttered, "Thanks."

"Gee. Does that mean I get to stay and play with you for a while?" she asked lightly.

He grinned over at her and kept driving. This was rapidly turning into a most interesting assignment.

Chapter 3

The terrain outside was flat and treeless, a black expanse under a moonless, cloudless sky. When summer came, it would be crisscrossed by sloughs and streams and teeming with mosquitoes. Not another sign of humanity was visible in any direction. Misty watched her travelling companion closely as she casually tossed out, "Just out of curiosity, do you know where this road goes?"

"Does it matter? It's the only road and I had to get out of there."

It was little more than a set of parallel ruts, truth be told. They'd be lucky if it wasn't washed out from the spring break-up of ice. "What's so dangerous about Camp Green that you had to run like this? That nurse is no longer a threat."

He threw her a dark look, made even darker by the dim glow of the dashboard casting his features into red light and black shadow. "Where there's one sleeper agent, there's always another."

"Let me guess. You think I'm the other sleeper, just hanging out in the middle of nowhere, waiting for you to steal a MiG and show up in the wilds of western Alaska." He started and she tsked. "Such hubris, Vasily."

He frowned at the road. "There were CIA agents and at least one Russian operative at the camp. Why not more?"

"Good point." She paused. Then added, "Honestly, it must have been pure luck that your government happened to have a man at Camp Green whom it could activate so quickly."

"Russia is not my government," he snapped.

She made a show of surprise. "Really? Then you're not a Russian military test pilot?"

"I didn't say that."

He glanced over at her, and their gazes locked. Heat built instantly in the confines of the jeep.

"Who are you?" he countered.

She was wise to his technique. Ask a question to send the conversation off in another direction whenever she got too close to a nerve. That was okay. She'd come back to the subject of who he really was later.

"I wondered when you'd get around to asking that. My friends call me Misty. I'm a U.S. Air Force pilot. I flew a general up to the camp to observe a training exercise this morning. I was supposed to stay for a couple days while he plays with the boys and then fly him out." Somehow, mentioning the fact that she was also a Special Forces operative didn't seem likely to inspire trust in her companion.

"How long have you been flying?" he fired at her.

Ever since the accident. Nearly fifteen years ago, now. Hard to believe it has been that long. "I've been in the air force for ten years. I did a little flying before that, too."

"Where are you stationed?"

"Washington, D.C." It was, in fact, where the Joint Special Operations Command—the Medusas' employer—was partially headquartered. The Medusas spent most of their stateside time training at other facilities around the country, but why split hairs?

"You're not telling me something," he announced.

She laughed lightly. "There's lots I'm not telling you. But then, I expect there's lots you're not telling me, either. Half the attraction of a person is the mystery of him, don't you think?"

The jeep swerved a bit. He steadied it and then looked over at her. "Are you flirting with me?"

"Would you mind if I were?"

That silenced him. Let him chew on that. If he wanted to play head games, she was happy to oblige. She hadn't grown up swimming in the shark-infested waters of high society for nothing.

Eventually, he asked, "So where does this road go?"

One of his more feeble attempts at a misdirect, but she'd play along. "To Bethel."

"How far away is this Bethel place?"

"About a hundred miles. Assuming the road is still there."

That garnered an alarmed look out of him. "And if it isn't?"

"Then we get to wait for a boat or a float plane to come along and pick us up. After that, the options get interesting."

"Like what?"

"Well, you and I could hike a really long ways. Although, with your leg needing to mend, that could be a problem. Or, we could spend a few weeks waiting for the road to dry out…hmm. I like that one. Stranded in the wilderness together. Sounds romantic, doesn't it? How would we ever occupy all that time?"

His eyes popped wide open and then narrowed sharply. "Are you a sparrow?" he demanded.

Sparrow was vernacular for female spies willing to sleep with their targets in the line of duty. Her Medusa training hadn't included even a hint of such a requirement. "Are you serious! Those teeny little mosquito eaters? Couldn't you compare me to something majestic like a swan? Or maybe a falcon? They're swift and beautiful and always get their prey."

"Don't play with fire, Misty Cordell. You could get burned."

He was warning her off him? The idea was laughable.

"I live for danger." And that was probably the most truthful thing she'd said to him so far. Her family accused her of having a death wish. What they didn't seem to grasp was that she chased adrenaline in order to feel alive.

"What? No more witty repartee?" he needled.

Her gaze narrowed. Time for a little topic shift of her own. "Tell me about this black box I rescued. What is it?"

"That's none of your concern."

She replied lightly, "If we're going to be partners in crime you really *must* work on trusting me more."

"We're *not* partners!"

"You need me, whether you like it or not, flyboy."

That got a good glare out of him. She laughed in his face. Which seemed to throw him. He drove on in silence. She noticed that periodically he reached down to rub his thigh. The wound must be smarting after running around on it and getting bumped around like this over rocks and ruts. "Let me drive for a while. You need to rest your leg. And speaking of which, I bet this vehicle has a first aid kit in it somewhere. Maybe there's a little morphine in it."

"They hit me with a painkiller earlier. I'm okay for now."

"Still, you're hurt. You should let me drive."

"And how do I know you won't turn around and drive right back to Camp Green?"

"You don't. I guess you'd better not fall asleep, then. But I can tell your leg hurts. Come sit over here and prop it up on the dashboard. You know it'll feel better."

He slowed the jeep and stopped it. She hopped out of its warm interior and into the night's sharp chill, heading around back of the vehicle. He had to be freezing in just those shorts and a T-shirt. He met her behind the car in the red glow of the taillights. She stopped. Looked up at him. His sex appeal slammed into her, a tangible thing hovering between them. He carried himself with innate class—a cleanly sculpted elegance of form and function. He was roughly six inches taller than she, which put him at around six feet two. She guessed his age at around forty or late thirties after some hard living. He stared down at her.

The tension built between them, climbing to nearly violent proportions. Part lust and part pissing contest, the combination was incendiary. She leaned toward him infinitesimally, and he mirrored the faint sway. Either he was attracted to her, too, or he was one subtle operator. Either way, he was dangerous.

"Right, then," she drew back sharply and stepped around him. His mental head shake was clear as a bell. *Good.* Off balance, right where she wanted him. He startled her, though, by grabbing her arm and spinning her around. He crowded her, backing her up against the jeep's fender. He braced a hand on either side of her head against the rear window.

"I don't know what your game is, but be careful around me, little girl."

He had *no idea* what she was capable of. She highly doubted he posed any serious threat to her and her deadly Medusa training. She was proficient in all kinds of hand-to-hand combat techniques…and practiced them regularly. Sometimes even with her life on the line.

Menace radiated from him. And damned if it didn't make her blood sing. She stared up at him, her chest rising and falling rapidly. His gaze dropped below her neck and climbed again, slowly. Fire flickered in the black recesses of his gaze.

She breathed up at him, "Who are you, really? You didn't tell those CIA agents the truth, did you? What's your name?"

He spun away from her and stumbled. Her hands shot out to grab his arm and steady him. She registered chiseled muscle in his upper arm. *Whoa.*

He growled, "Get in the car and drive."

Greg climbed into the passenger side of the car warily. His leg was killing him, but he'd die before he admitted it to the beautiful American agent. A fascinating woman, Misty Cordell. She had a certain…playful…quality. As if she didn't quite take any of this seriously. It was shocking and refreshing after the past five years. To have lived in the skin of another man for so long, a Russian spymaster no less, had been a tremendous strain.

He closed his eyes, and that horrendous night took form around him once more.

They'd been sitting in a café, waiting for the hand-off. A Russian Army officer was supposed to walk in, give him a pre-arranged numeric code, and then he'd un-handcuff Nemorov and turn him over to his own government.

Except when a man in a Russian Army uniform walked in, he'd pulled out an AK-47 and unloaded it into Nemorov. The sound was deafening. People had screamed and dived for cover, and glass and chairs went flying everywhere. He'd been sprayed in blood. So damned much blood. He couldn't even tell if any of it was his own. He hadn't felt any bullets hit him. But in the adrenaline of the moment, he couldn't be sure.

He'd pulled his own pistol and fired back, shooting the army man twice in the torso. The guy turned around and stumbled out of the café, but ominously, he'd stopped in the doorway and waved his arm as if gesturing for back-ups to join him.

They had to get out of here!

He'd grabbed Nemorov around the waist and hauled the unconscious spy back toward the kitchen. The owner hollered at him to get out, brandishing a butcher knife. Right. Like a knife was going to do a hill of beans of good against the Kalashnikovs on their way in the front door.

He'd shouted back, asking for a rear exit, and the owner had screamed that there was none.

He'd looked around in a panic. Spotted a heavy metal door. The freezer. Crap. There was no other cover to be had. He had to get the damned handcuffs off to stand a chance of getting out of here alive. Nemorov was starting to choke on his own blood, his breath rattling loudly in his chest. The guy was bleeding heavily from at least a half-

dozen gunshot wounds, his shirt and pants soaked black
with blood.

He'd hauled the dying spy into the meat locker and
yanked the door shut behind them. A mop stood just inside
the door and he used it to wedge the door handle shut.
Frantically, he'd dug in his pocket for the handcuff key.
He fumbled with the cuffs, which were slippery with
Nemorov's blood. God, the guy was bleeding like a stuck
pig. How could he have lost so much blood and still be
alive?

The handcuff finally snapped free and fell away from
the Russian's wrist. Greg pulled the metal bracelet off his
own hand and flung it aside. He looked around for another
way out. No ceiling vent. Damn. Maybe he could shoot
his way out through the back wall. It should back up onto
a side street. He pressed his ear against the wall and
pounded on it with his fist. It sounded as solid as a bank
vault.

Someone yanked at the freezer door. The shooters were
here. He looked around desperately for a hiding place. He
tested the metal shelves, stacked with boxes of food and
liquor. Sturdy enough to hold his weight.

He climbed fast, wedging himself in on the top shelf
behind paper bags of rolls and bread he hastily pulled in
front of himself. The mop handle cracked. Broke in half
with a loud splintering sound. The door burst open.

He held his breath, his shoulders pressed against the icy
wall of his hiding spot. Four armed men rushed inside. The
first man pointed an AK-47 at Nemorov's prone body
while another man squatted down and checked for a pulse.

The crouching man announced, *"Myertvuh."* Dead.

Crap. His mission was completely blown. The gunmen
backed out of the freezer. Silence fell around him and the

smell of blood congealed in his nostrils. Only the humming of the freezer unit vibrated in the stillness. He lay there until he was shivering so violently he feared he wouldn't be able to climb down.

He half rolled, half fell to the floor. His feet stung as though a thousand needles were being stabbed into them as he landed. He blew on his fingers to warm them, and stumbled over to the dead man's body, which was already growing stiff. Whether from rigor mortis or freezing, he couldn't tell.

Now what the hell was he supposed to do? The CIA hadn't briefed him on this contingency. He searched the dead man, taking his wallet, watch and class ring from Moscow State University. He opened the guy's Russian passport. Maybe there was some sort of government phone number in it somewhere where he could report this guy's death.

In the distance, he heard the rise and fall of a police siren.

He stopped, arrested by the guy's photo. He hadn't noticed it before, but he himself bore a more-than-passing resemblance to Nemorov. The similarity, particularly in the picture, was startling. He could almost pass for the guy.

And that was when he'd hatched his plan. What if he pretended to be Nemorov? He'd been the guy's primary interrogator over the past six months. He knew more about the guy's life than anyone on the planet except Nemorov himself. Not only had Nemorov been highly placed within the Russian Security Service, but the guy had extensive ties with the Russian mafia. It could be tremendously informative to live the guy's life for a while.

Nemorov had been in the United States for nearly five years undercover. Any anomalies in behavior or memory would be easy to explain away. And what an amazing opportunity to infiltrate the very highest levels of the Russian intelligence community!

He'd switched wallets and passports with the dead Russian, taken off his own watch, and slipped on Nemorov's ring and watch. And in that moment, he'd become Vasily Nemorov.

He'd watched for an opening to contact the Americans, to let them know he was alive and operating undercover in Russia, but the security around the offices Nemorov had worked in was incredible. He'd dared not take the risk of contacting the Americans.

After a few months in Moscow, he'd run into a CIA report of the death of one Greg Mitchell in a shootout with the Russian mafia. And then it wasn't so urgent to contact the Americans. They thought he was dead. He settled into his new identity and started gathering information for the day when he was ready to leave.

Nemorov had been one of the highest level analysts in the Russian intelligence community. His job had been to look for exploitable weak spots in the lives and personalities of important individuals around the world. The haul of information was breathtaking. And Greg squirreled every bit of it away in an encrypted file on a portable hard drive that never left his possession.

He'd lived in the skin of another man until he'd actually gotten comfortable in it.

And he'd waited.

It had been the Russian mafia that finally forced his hand. Nemorov had used the mafia for occasional side jobs and tips, and the day came when the mafia finally called in their chit. Greg was not prepared to assassinate the Russian Minister of Finance in order to maintain his cover. It was time to go.

He'd arranged for a trip to a Russian air force base in eastern Siberia, and had finagled a couple rides in a MiG simulator. Then he'd stolen the fastest jet the Russians had, and here he was. On a desolate road in the middle of the night in the middle of nowhere. He was on American soil and with the most beautiful woman he'd ever laid eyes on. It was a hell of a twist of fate.

For the first time in five years, he relaxed.

Misty watched her companion closely. He was lost in thought for some time, any number of emotions flitting across his face. And none of them looked like easy or comfortable emotions. *What was he thinking about?*

Eventually, he let out a long, slow breath and leaned his head against the backrest. His eyes drifted closed. *Finally. He'd relaxed.* Time to throw him off balance again.

She commented, "We make a great team, you know. I can tell you're a player." The word had the same double connotation in Russian, and with his perfect command of the language, she had no doubt he'd catch her play on words.

His eyes snapped open and his head jerked upright. "What in hell does that mean?" Tension abruptly rolled off him.

She smiled over at him knowingly. "You don't have to play innocent with me. Haven't you ever heard you can't con a con artist?"

Something akin to shock flashed through his gaze before it snapped forward, pinned unseeingly to the track stretching away in the dark before them. Her interrogation training had never covered this particular technique for getting inside a person's head, but her instinct said to go with it. He'd spot anything less obtuse in a heartbeat.

He remained wired after that, staring silently ahead.

The rough road held up all the way to Bethel, and they arrived in town shortly before midnight. It was an oddball collection of homes ranging from modest conventional to outright eccentric. Unemployment was high in this part of the state, and the ragged texture of the town reflected it. She pulled into the parking lot of Bethel's lone hotel, a mostly log structure, and according to a sign by the front door, a supporter of the annual Ca'Mai Native American dance festival and each winter's Kuskokwim 300 dogsled race.

"What are you doing?" Greg asked in alarm.

"Getting us a room for the night."

"We have to keep going. They'll come after us!"

"There are no more roads. The only way in or out of Bethel is by air or boat. We'll have to wait until morning to get out of here."

He stared at her in disbelief. "Are you joking?"

"Ask the hotel manager if you don't believe me."

Greg stomped in after her, muttering about this being car-crazy America, for God's sake, and how couldn't there be roads to everywhere?

The night manager, a wide-faced and taciturn Inuit—the Yup'ik tribe dominated this region—came to the counter after they rang the bell several times.

"We'd like a room, please," Misty asked with a warm smile for him.

The manager thawed considerably. "What brings you to these parts?"

"Just passing through. We were out camping and lost our gear in a break-up. We need to get back to Anchorage."

"The ice, it be mean this time of year. Lucky you didn't lose your lives."

"That's what I told my husband."

The manager handed over a key to her and pointed to which side of the building the room was on while Vasily-Greg picked up a handful of brochures from a display by the counter.

Misty asked, "Is there a sporting goods or clothing place in town? My husband could use some pants."

The manager laughed, "Over on Third Street. Mike opens his place up 'long about ten in the morning if he's not too hung over."

Misty grinned. "Thanks."

Greg just scowled.

She drove them around the side of the building to their room. While she unlocked the door, he wrestled the blackened box out of the jeep and carried it in behind her. She made another trip out to the jeep to see what it had by way of supplies. Cop cars generally carried a pretty good stash of utility equipment, and occasionally weapons. This one didn't produce any guns, but it had a full complement of arctic survival gear. She snagged a couple things she might need before morning and headed inside.

Greg was examining the black box. He straightened sharply when she came in.

"Still not gonna tell me what that is?" she asked.

"No. However, I will tell you this. It needs a battery charge in the next day or so."

Time to hit him with the helpless blond-who's-confused-by-all-that-complicated-electronics act. "Whatever for?"

"There's a self-destruct mechanism inside this. If its battery runs out of power, it'll be triggered."

It wasn't hard to fake opening her eyes wide in surprise. *What in the world* was *that thing?* No aircraft black box would ever have a self-destruct in it! The very point was for the record to survive until it was found and read. "Then I guess we need to head for Anchorage. It'll have an electronics or computer store for you to get whatever that gizmo needs."

He shrugged, thumbing through the brochures. She spotted a picture of a Cessna float plane. Damn. He was plotting his escape. Ten-to-one he was planning to ditch her and run with the black box. She'd see about that.

She made a warp-speed trip to the restroom—after all, she still had the jeep key. When she emerged—thankful that he was still in the room—she asked, "Are you hungry? I found some energy bars in the back of the jeep."

"No, thanks."

She shrugged out of her flight jacket and unzipped her boots. "Hope you don't mind sharing the bed with me. I promise to keep all my clothes on." A pause. "Tonight."

Humor actually glinted in his eyes for a moment. Without comment, he turned off the light and stretched out on the bed beside her. She gave him a moment to get comfortable, and then she reached out in the dark and slapped his left wrist with the metal object cupped in her hand.

He jerked upright. "What in hell did you just do?" He reached out to his side of the bed and turned on a lamp.

She lifted her right wrist, displaying the handcuffs stretching between their two hands. "A little insurance to make sure you're still here in the morning."

Outrage lent his voice vibrato. "You *handcuffed* me to you?"

"Clever, aren't I?" she answered perkily.

He glared at her for several seconds, then his scowl dissolved into laughter. "You're incorrigible."

"Why, thank you. That's the nicest thing you've ever

said to me." He turned off the light. The bed shifted as he flopped back down. "Sweet dreams, Vasily."

"Get some sleep."

Except, sleep stubbornly eluded her. The man lying tensely beside her was impossible to ignore, as was her reaction to him. He stirred her senses and made her feel nearly as alive as she did when she was flinging a supersonic jet through space. Or when she was getting shot at, she admitted to herself wryly. And that should probably be a warning to her about her misplaced attraction to a defector cum spy.

"I'm busy, Gennady. What is it?"

"Some news, General. The MiG is destroyed. Our missile hit it dead-on. However, our man was not successful in his mission to eliminate Nemorov."

"What happened?" General Karkarov asked sharply.

"I have no details. But our inside man is dead, and Nemorov is nowhere to be found. Apparently, he has fled the military base."

The general steepled his fingers in front of his mouth for a moment. "That may not be such a disaster. If he is running, Nemorov cannot be debriefed. As long as he's not talking to the American authorities, we are safe. Do we have any assets who can pick up his trail reasonably soon?"

Gennady shrugged. "Where there's enough money, there are always available assets."

"Get someone on his tail. And keep the pressure on him. I want him running too hard to stop and talk."

"Yes, sir."

"And Gennady?"

"Yes?"

"Tell our next man to be sure not to kill him. Not yet. Not until the time is right."

"Yes, sir."

Chapter 4

Misty semi-awoke, more unconscious than conscious. Something heavy lay across her. Something pressing her deliciously into the mattress and arousing erotic sensations deep in her core. Warm breath ruffled a stray tendril of her hair, tickling her ear. Slabs of ribs covered in muscle flexed under her fingertips. She shifted slightly, and a big, hard, masculine body stretched with the power of a big cat against hers.

"Mmm," a male voice sighed in contentment.

She shot all the way past full consciousness to combat ready.

Lips moved seductively against her neck. "Dobroye utra." Good morning.

Whoa. She lurched, attempting to slide out from under him. But her arm didn't go anywhere. And since her body was attached to it, neither did she. Metal rattled.

"Ouch!" the male voice complained.

Of course. The handcuffs. Greg.

The world abruptly did a one-eighty roll, and his surrounding weight left her all of a sudden. She subsided, relaxing against the warmth of the mattress…until she realized that wasn't mattress entirely. She half-lay on top of Greg, one of her legs draped over his, her thigh nestled intimately against an entirely male bulge. She lurched away again, and only managed to wrench her shoulder painfully. Her hand stayed firmly where it was and she remained sprawled across his chest. Okay, so maybe handcuffing them together hadn't been such a great idea.

"Next time, handcuff both our right hands together," he murmured in amusement. "Then we'll be able to spoon against each other and sleep more comfortably."

She scowled over at him.

"Good morning to you, too." He laughed back.

No doubt about it. His Russian accent sounded native to her. Yet, the CIA men said he was American. Very few Americans ever mastered that perfect an accent, even if they had lived in Russia for several years like him.

As for the CIA's claim that he wasn't a pilot, he clearly knew enough to take off and land a supersonic jet. It was something that could be learned in a simulator with some qualified instruction and a little practice, but how had he managed to get access to simulators and training if he *wasn't* a Russian military pilot? Was he really a CIA spy at all? Heck, was he even American? Why would the CIA agents lie to her?

She snorted to herself over that thought. Why *wouldn't* they? That bunch saw circles within circles, conspiracies within conspiracies. No telling what their convoluted thought processes might be.

She indulged briefly in a fantasy of what it would be like if Greg rolled over and made love to her. Unfortunately, her imagination was pretty good, and hot discomfort flooded her at being handcuffed to a Hollywood-beautiful man of mystery. She closed her eyes, concentrating on banishing the improper images from her mind. But then the world rolled over again. Her eyes popped open, and Cary Grant's alter ego gazed down at her, smiling a good morning.

"Let's try this again," he murmured. "Hi, beautiful."

A response fell out of her mouth without thought. "Hi, handsome."

His grin widened and those killer dimples flashed again. "So. How are we going to manage bathroom visits in our current state?"

She considered for a moment. "If you give me your word of honor you won't ditch me, I'll unlock us."

That seemed to give him pause. But then he said, "All right. My word of honor—if you'll give me yours that you won't look at or touch the computer while I'm in the shower."

A computer, eh? Do tell.

"Your word on it?" he pressed.

Drat. Her word was something she took seriously. It mattered in her world. Lives rode on people doing what they said they would…or not doing what they said they wouldn't. She sighed. "Okay. Fine. I won't mess with the computer, and you won't run away. Do we have a deal?"

"Deal."

"Yippee," she muttered. "Détente lives."

They both sat up and turned for their own side of the bed. And pulled up short as the handcuffs wrenched at their arms. Laughing, she gestured at the foot of the bed. "Shall we head for neutral territory?"

They both got on their knees and teetered toward the end of the bed. The mattress was old and springy, and they ended up falling in a heap. He twisted to land on the bottom, and she fell on top of his chest.

The effect on her was electric. The breath ripped out of her lungs, shredding her reserve and stripping away all semblance of civilized thought. Alarmed by the violence of her sexual reaction, she clamped down hard on her urge to writhe against him from neck to toes.

Almost accidentally, her gaze met his. She forced hers not to slide away in embarrassment. "So. Are you just being a gentleman and cushioning my fall, or are you flirting with me this time?"

"Does it matter which?"

Oh, geez. His voice was a silky murmur that drew her in and melted her as surely as summer in Siberia.

She summoned what little composure she could and replied breathlessly, "Being a gentleman is possibly even more attractive to me than being a gorgeous flirt, so I'd have to say both work."

"Glad to hear it," he murmured. All sorts of untoward parts of them bumped into each other as they clumsily achieved a sitting position. At one point she nearly ended up in his lap, wrecking what little equanimity she'd regained.

That smile of his should be registered as a lethal weapon. She dug the handcuff key out of the pocket of her flight jacket and set them both free. And darned if she didn't miss his presence beside her, the back of his hand bumping into hers, his heat wrapping around her.

Regardless of their deal, she still took the jeep key into the bathroom with her and was in and out of the shower in two minutes flat. She was a firm believer in trust…with vigilance.

Their stop at a local sporting goods store was extremely productive. They both purchased sturdy slacks, turtlenecks, sweaters and rugged hiking boots. She bought a backpack and tossed in basic camping gear and several boxes of ammunition for the Glock pistol she'd lifted off the dead "nurse."

Next they headed for Bethel Airport to rent a plane, which in these parts was nearly as easy as renting a car. Fortunately, one of her many aviation ratings was in a Cessna 172, and she happened to have flown one less than two weeks ago. Hence, she was current in the airplane type. She showed the fixed-base operator her pilot's license, and after exclaiming over her many other exotic aircraft ratings, he readily rented her a plane.

While she prepared and filed their flight plan to Anchorage, she tossed out several aviation-related questions that any pilot would know. Greg flunked every one. Any pilot about to fly over mountains would definitely care what the service ceiling of his aircraft was. And any instrument-rated pilot would know about positive-control airspace—the part of the sky over eighteen thousand feet where it was necessary to be under the control of aircraft controllers.

Maybe the CIA guys were being truthful about him, after all.

The flight to Anchorage yielded more interesting results. He had a basic grasp of keeping the plane level and turning to follow a certain heading, but he was clueless about reading navigation maps or setting up an elaborate instrument approach. She suggested smoothly that, given his injury and unfamiliarity with U.S. airspace, she should make the approach and landing. He didn't object.

"What sort of gear do you need to fix that box?" she

asked him as they stood in a phone booth with the Anchorage Yellow Pages open shortly after they landed .

"A variable voltage regulator with a universal plug system."

She frowned. "In other words, the local discount computer place isn't going to cut it. You need a real electronics store."

"Correct."

She thumbed down through the listings. "Here's one. It's not too far from here, I think."

"Nothing's too far from here," he retorted dryly.

"Hey, don't knock it. Anchorage is as good as it gets for a thousand miles in any direction by way of shopping. It's not my fault you didn't head for Los Angeles."

"Not enough fuel to make it that far, or believe me, I would have."

Smith and Jones said he'd been born and raised in southern California. She couldn't resist needling a bit. "You'd like L.A. Friendly place. Clean. Fun. Great highways."

He opened his mouth to say something, but shut it instead.

She grinned to herself. "C'mon. Let's go get you your thingamajiggies before that box blows up."

"It won't blow up. Acid foam will be released onto the surface of the hard drive and destroy all the stored information."

Hard drive, huh? And apparently, the information on it was important. But what sort of computer had a self-destruct mechanism built into it and required a specially regulated voltage to power its battery? Sounded like one heck of a secure computer. Which begged the question, what was stored on it that he was being so secretive about?

Why not just download everything from the hard drive onto a storage disk and haul out the files in his back pocket?

She drove the grid layout of Anchorage streets and found the place they were looking for in a few minutes. It wasn't a big store, but when they stepped inside, the array of gadgets and electronic parts cramming the walls and display racks was impressive.

It turned out the Russian and English words for most of the gear he required were pretty much the same, so Greg and the store clerk had no trouble communicating.

She wandered the aisles on her own, amazed at what she could buy in there. With the addition of a few simple chemicals, she could put together a hefty improvised explosive device out of this place. She'd just paused in front of a display of lenses and telescopes when a loud noise made her flinch hard.

Glass crashed to the ground as the store's front window exploded into a thousand pieces. She ducked, running in a weaving path toward the far side of the store and the checkout register where Greg and the clerk were pinned down. Both men lay on the floor, and she dived to her belly beside them.

"Did you hear shots?" she panted in Russian.

"No. The shooter's using a silencer."

"You're sure there's a shooter?"

He pointed up at the wall behind the register. A ragged, round hole in the wood wall pronounced without a shadow of a doubt the type of attack they were under. She reached for the Glock in her coat pocket.

Greg rolled to his side, bumping into her shooting arm, and swore under his breath. Fortunately, the safety was still on the weapon. But then he jumped to his feet, swearing freely now. She craned to look around the end of the counter to see what had him so tense. It was a woman. A customer, frozen in place in the middle of the store, staring in blank shock at the mess that had just been the storefront.

Ping.

Another shot struck something metal off to Misty's right, not far from where Greg had just been.

"He's still shooting!" she called out in Russian. She pointed the Glock toward the front of the store, but as of yet, had no target in sight.

"Get down, ma'am!" Greg hollered in unaccented English. "Lie down on the floor. *Now.*"

The woman turned slowly to stare at him.

Totally panicked. Vapor-locked brain. Damn. Misty pushed to a crouch, preparing to sprint over and tackle the poor woman. But Greg beat her to it. He dived for the woman's waist, rolled onto his back and carried her down to the ground on top of him, just as another metallic ping sounded somewhere near the back wall. *Nice move.*

And nice English.

"Get her out of here," she called out in English. "You two crawl for the back of the store. I'm going to work my way up front and lay down covering fire."

Greg shot her a thumbs-up as she made her way forward. She propped the Glock on a low display stand just inside the remnants of the front window. Thankfully, no pedestrians were in her field of fire, whether by luck or by virtue of hearing shots fired and fleeing.

"Slide me some binoculars," she called to the clerk.

The man reached up fast to the wall beside the register and grabbed a pair, doing as she said and sliding them toward her. She had to use her foot to fetch them when they stopped short of her, but in a moment, she was peering outside, quartering the view into discrete search areas. The shooter would have to show himself eventually. Either he'd move or she'd catch a muzzle flash.

It was a muzzle flash that zeroed her in on her target. The roof of a building one door down and across the street. At this relatively close range, the optical resolution was outstanding. He'd come up again, and she'd get a great look at him…and a great shot.

Sure enough, a black baseball cap came up first, several feet to the right of his last location. A larger-than-life face appeared in her round, magnified field of view. A fragment of the wood window frame exploded not a foot in front of her face. He ducked down out of sight once more just as she dived for the floor.

Holy crap! She *knew* that face.

She almost dropped the binoculars. *Agent Smith.* Of Camp Green CIA fame. And the sonofabitch was shooting at her! She set aside the field glasses and settled herself in a prone shooting position. A Glock wasn't her ideal weapon—it didn't have the punch to make a certain takedown even if she hit dead-on, but it was all she had. Still, it was only a thirty-yard shot. She never missed at that range.

Her thoughts churned as she waited for Smith to reappear. Was he the other Russian sleeper Greg had worried about? Or had the CIA sanctioned a hit on Greg? Why would they want to kill their own man? It made no sense. *Either way, nobody shoots at me and lives to tell about it, thank you very much.*

It was over in a matter of seconds. When Smith popped up to shoot, she prayed her sights were true and took her shot. She nailed him in the chest. The force of the bullet's impact snapped his body back and he fell over, out of sight.

She jumped up and raced through the store, slipping and sliding on shards of glass. She burst into the back storeroom. The woman he'd rescued huddled behind Greg.

"Are you two okay?" Misty bit out in Russian.

"Yes. You?" he replied in the same language.

"I'm fine. We've got to get out of here. The police will be here any second."

He nodded tersely and leaped up.

"Do you have everything you need?" Misty asked.

"It's all in a couple of bags by the cash register."

They bolted out of the storeroom, grabbed the white plastic bags and sprinted from the store. Misty's gunshots had caused a furor and people ran every which way. It was great cover for them to make their own escape. They hustled to their rental car and drove away amid the general uproar. They passed the first police car two blocks from the electronics store.

"We've got to ditch this car," he announced.

"Can you hot-wire anything besides jeeps?"

He nodded. "Take your pick."

"Let's head for a grocery store. Nobody will notice a car parked in the lot for a while. Good selection of cars, too."

They pulled into a grocery store lot and Greg pointed out a seven- or eight-year old SUV. "How about that one? It shouldn't have a tricky alarm system."

Misty nodded and parked a little ways from it. After a quick look around the parking lot, she pulled a Slim Jim— a tool for popping car door locks—out of her backpack and passed it to Greg.

"What are you doing with one of those?"

"I lifted it out of the military police jeep last night. I thought it might come in handy."

"You thought right," he muttered as he popped the door

lock. He crawled under the dashboard, and with the help of the wire cutters and needle-nosed pliers Misty passed him, had the car running in under a minute.

"Man, you're good at that," she commented. "I know a few folks who'd love to take lessons from you."

"I bet. Get in."

She tossed their gear in the back seat and climbed in the passenger side. "Let's ride, Clyde."

"Roger that, Bonnie."

Okay, no Russian should know the Bonnie and Clyde reference. And even though they'd reverted to speaking Russian, his English back in the store to that lady had been flawless. He'd also responded without hesitation when she'd shouted instructions at him in English. He was definitely American or had spent a lot of time living in America.

So. He wasn't a pilot, and he possibly wasn't Russian. Did that mean the third thing the CIA men had told her was also accurate? Was he a spy for the CIA?

If so, why in the *hell* had they just tried to kill their own man?

Chapter 5

Panic practically crushed Greg's heart. How in the hell had one of his enemies caught up with him so fast? He hadn't been entirely surprised by the attempted hit on him at the American military base. He knew the Russians had various assets inside the Special Forces community.

But on the open streets of Anchorage, Alaska? That was another matter entirely.

Who was the shooter?

The Russian air force? Nah, not likely. The Russian military wasn't that efficient any more. The Russian mafia? Filled with former KGB agents and equipped with the latest high-tech gear, they were as good or better than any western army. But why would they come after him so quickly and so aggressively? They'd asked him to kill a high-ranking Russian official and he'd turned them down. That wasn't cause to pursue him a continent away and try to assassinate him.

That left the Russian government. Although the glory days of the Soviet Union were long gone, the remaining regime was still formidable, particularly when well and truly ticked off. The plan was to fly to Alaska and make contact with the CIA—and invoke its protection as quickly as possible. Only the American government was up to the task of protecting him from the Russians.

But when the military base had shown itself to be compromised, he'd snagged a jeep and fled with the intent to head for the civilian United States and the full protection of U.S. law enforcement agencies. The attack in Anchorage was disturbing because the American system had failed to protect him.

He jerked his attention back to the car. He was going too fast. The last thing they needed was to draw any police attention to them after fleeing the scene of a shooting. And if the paleness around Misty's mouth and her general seriousness were any indication, someone had died back there.

He eased off the accelerator and matched his speed to the flow of traffic around him, several miles per hour above the speed limit. Not too fast, not too slow. Just blending in with traffic in a way guaranteed not to get him a ticket. His adrenaline was proving a challenge to corral, however. If he didn't know better, he'd say his famous nerves of steel had deserted him.

As they approached the Seward Highway intersection, Misty glanced over at him. "North or south? Shall we lose ourselves in the vastness of Denali or head for civilization?"

As tempting as it was to simply lose himself in the wilds of Alaska and never emerge again, he had a plan. He'd go ahead with it, come hell or high water. He replied, "I have to make a stop in Vancouver."

"Why Vancouver?"

"I have something to pick up there."

"What is it?"

He winced. The less she knew, the better.

"Soon," she murmured. "Very soon, we're going to sit down and have a Talk. Capital T. I want some straight answers, and I'm not backing down until I get them."

"I think we would both agree that while driving down the highway in a stolen car is not the time for it," he remarked.

Thankfully, she remained silent. For now.

The police would expect them to head east on the Glenn Highway and then south toward the lower forty-eight, or north on the Park Highway toward Denali. So, instead, he guided the vehicle due south on the Seward Highway, which took them further out the peninsula at whose neck Anchorage perched. It was all about being unpredictable.

They drove for a few minutes, and then a sound from the back seat startled him. It was muffled, but definitely the ring of a cell phone.

Misty smacked herself on the forehead and exclaimed, "Of course! That's how they found us!"

Ahh. She must have one of those phones with a Global Positioning System locator chip in it. He should've taken the damned thing away from her the minute he agreed to let her come with him on this little junket. *Sloppy*.

Misty unbuckled her seatbelt and reached into the back seat to find her phone. It afforded him a rather provocative view of her backside, but in the name of being a gentleman, he did his best not to stare. She twisted around, collapsing back into her seat, and answered the phone.

He listened unabashedly to the one-sided conversation.

"Hi, sir…Fine…No, sir…Yup…Nope…Yup."

A pause. Then, she said matter-of-factly, "Yes I do. I

did it. He tried to kill Vasily. I jumped on him and we struggled for the weapon. It discharged and hit him. And speaking of which, have the contents of the syringe the guy had on him been analyzed?"

Who was she talking to that she'd freely admit to shooting someone? She'd called the person 'sir.' Her supervisor, maybe? He couldn't imagine telling one of his Russian superiors so casually that he'd shot someone. The paperwork to follow would have been mind-numbing.

Misty spoke again. "The guy claimed to be there to give Vasily medication, but Vasily told me he'd had all the injections he was supposed to get for the night already. When Vasily declined to take the injection, the assailant pulled out a Glock."

Another pause while she listened.

Then she continued, "One more thing for you, sir. Ask the CIA why its man tried to kill Vasily a couple of hours ago in Anchorage."

What?

The CIA—

Tried to kill—

Him? But he was *their* man!

He actually heard the exclamation from the other end of the phone.

"Yes, sir. I'm positive. I saw his face before I pulled the trigger. It was definitely one of the CIA agents who took me to talk to Vasily."

The two guys who'd come to see him in his hospital room had shown him their Central Intelligence Agency IDs. He'd examined the credentials closely, and they were authentic. And they'd told him the Agency was delighted that he was still alive. That they were looking forward to hearing his full debrief and seeing the files he'd brought out with him. They'd told him to get some rest, take it easy overnight, and they'd start the debrief the next day.

And instead, one of those men had tried to *kill* him?

His breath came short and fast. What in bloody hell was he supposed to do now? He'd been counting on the CIA to protect him from the various Russian factions. *Was he out in the cold completely without a net?*

And just who was Misty Cordell? How did she figure into all this?

This meant he was truly alone now. For the past five years he'd lived in secrecy and isolation, but he'd always had the comforting knowledge that an entire government was behind him. Uncle Sam would welcome him with open arms whenever he chose to end his self-imposed exile in the wilderness. Never, in his wildest dreams, had he imagined this sort of homecoming.

He'd made his choice. He'd chosen to be American. But America had rejected him. Which meant he was a man without a country. Without a home. Without an identity to call his own.

He realized he was about to drive off the road, and he swerved the SUV back onto the highway. Was she one of them? Was she CIA? But if so, why had she shot the CIA man? Who was she working for? He hadn't had a chance to talk with her since the incident in the electronics store, other than to coordinate the details of their escape.

They needed to have a Talk, indeed.

He could see it now. They'd sit down, stare fixedly at each other, and neither one of them would say a word. They'd both be too busy hiding their own secrets to initiate a real conversation.

He was relieved to hear Misty's phone power down as

she clicked it shut. He'd have hated to mug her for her phone, but no way was he letting her leave it turned on so more CIA agents could track them down.

He blurted, "Are you sure the shooter was agency?"

She nodded grimly. "Dead certain."

Sonofabitch.

Misty watched Greg drive. Ever since he'd asked her to confirm the identity of the shooter in Anchorage, he'd been staring ahead grimly and gripping the steering wheel as though he was trying to strangle it.

She occupied herself mentally with listing out all the questions in need of answering, then dividing them into the ones Greg needed to answer and the ones she could work on herself.

Foremost on the latter list was where to go. Greg wanted to get to Vancouver. The obvious course of action would be to drive east to the Alaska Highway and then south. They could stop now to ditch their vehicle and acquire a new one, either by theft or rental. Both were ridiculously easy to track, though. She opened the glove compartment and rooted around among old receipts, napkins and assorted junk. Bingo. A map. She pulled it out and unfolded it across her lap.

They should have no trouble catching a southbound ferry somewhere along the coast. Southeastern Alaska's primary mode of transport was by sea. Although, if the various police agencies down the coast hadn't already been notified by the Anchorage police to be on the lookout for them, they would be soon. She traced their current route with her finger on the map, looking for small towns on the coast of the Seward Peninsula.

She checked her watch. They probably had two more

hours before the police net would kick into high gear. They had to be off the road by then. She picked three likely spots where they could ditch the SUV and skipped the first two. Might as well not make the police's job too easy.

"When we get to Whittier, let's get off the highway," she said.

"Then what?"

"Then we go to ground. If someone wants to kill us, I don't plan on making it easy to find us. From here on out, we become invisible."

He gave her a grim smile. "I like the way you think."

Wittenauer hung up the phone and cursed under his breath, a rare crack in his professional demeanor. Misty's ominous last words rang in his ear. *Tell the powers that be to back off. Give us some room. If they want to force us to act like criminals, we will. But I'd rather sort this thing out peacefully if we can.*

He'd told her to stay in touch. But in her current situation, he wasn't at all sure she'd heed that advice. And he couldn't entirely blame her. Special operators had a tendency to get real jumpy when multiple attempts were made on their lives in the space of less than a day.

He'd feel a whole lot better if she were surrounded by her teammates. Together, he figured the Medusas could think their way through just about anything. Although they were as physical as women came, it was their collective smarts that really set them apart and made them effective. It was also what made them so dangerous when they were cornered.

If that shooter in Anchorage really was CIA, he needed to get the Agency to back off of Misty, and back off *now,* if they didn't want to lose any more people.

* * *

Greg turned off at the exit Misty indicated, then asked, "Now what?" He felt like a wooden mannequin, going through the motions of existing right now. Thankfully, Misty seemed ready to take control of the decision-making.

"Now we hope we hit the tunnel at the right time."

Huh? "I beg your pardon?"

"Only way into Whittier is through a one-way tunnel. It reverses direction every hour."

Oh, for crying out loud. He muttered, "Quirky damned place, Alaska."

She laughed. "You should've squeezed a little extra fuel on your MiG and headed for California, I'm tellin' ya."

He just rolled his eyes at her.

They were lucky and hit the tunnel headed inbound to Whittier. From there it was a short drive to Prince William Sound and its gorgeous shoreline. Several piers were crowded with clustered fishing and pleasure boats.

"We need to find a garage of some kind to park this car in," Misty said.

Right. Hide the getaway car. They drove for a few minutes before Greg spotted a ramshackle barn half falling down. Winters were hard on structures in this part of the world. *Perfect.* He pulled inside the barn.

"Let's wipe this puppy down. May as well not make it easy for the cops to find us."

Thank God she was here. He was more or less non-functioning at the moment.

The Americans had tried to kill him!

The beginnings of outrage tickled around the edges of his shock.

The two of them efficiently wiped down the car's interior of fingerprints. While he pulled their gear out of the car, Misty removed the vehicle's license plates. She tossed them into her backpack while Greg wrestled the computer into the rucksack they'd bought earlier.

"Let's blow this pop stand," she translated into Russian.

He laughed. The line translated literally to, "Let's exhale on a frozen lollipop," but he caught her meaning. He followed her to the exit. They wrestled the half-rotten door mostly shut behind themselves. A few planks fell off, and they propped the gray pieces of wood against the door frame. From there, it was a short hike to the waterfront.

Misty murmured, "If I had enough time, I'd go into a saloon and eavesdrop on the locals for a while to find a mark."

He interjected, "Let me guess. Then you'd bat your eyelashes at him and flash a little cleavage, and he'd give us his boat."

She scowled at him. "Don't knock it. You can't believe the stuff men will do for a woman who shows an interest in them."

"Trust me. It has nothing to do with whether or not you're interested in them. I bet they fall all over themselves trying to get you to bed."

She snorted. "You don't know the half of it." A pause. "Or do you? You're a pretty good-looking guy. Do women paw all over you trying to get you in the sack?"

When he was out in public he was usually too focused on maintaining his Nemorov persona to pay much attention to it, but now that he thought about it, he nodded. "I guess so. I don't pay much attention to it, though."

She chuckled. "You must've driven Russian women

crazy. The pickings are slim enough over there for decent-looking, nice guys, but then to have you ignore them? They must have thought you were gay."

His gaze snapped to her. "I hope not!"

Her chuckle became a full-blown laugh.

He scanned the docks, looking for the right vessel to approach.

There. A seaworthy-looking, but otherwise dilapidated sport fishing boat, a small cabin cruiser in need of a paint job and new canvas awnings. Chipped gold paint declared it to be named the *Holy Mackerel.*

"What about that one over there?" He pointed, desperately hoping to distract her from the current conversation.

"Looks as good as any."

They strolled up to its mooring. "You're on, resident sex kitten. Do your stuff to the captain, eh?"

She rolled her eyes at him, then called, "Ahoy! Anyone aboard?"

No answer. She stuck out a foot and gave the corner of the boat a downward push. It rocked gently. "Anyone home?" she tried again.

A sleepy-eyed Inuit poked his head out of the below-deck quarters. Jet-black hair stood up all over his head and his ponytail was skewed to the side. He looked about twenty-five. A little young to have as much sailing experience as Greg was hoping for, but beggars couldn't be choosers.

"We need to go for a ride," Misty said. "A profitable one for you. No questions asked."

Greg was impressed. How did she hit that lilting tone of voice? It wasn't exactly flirtatious, but damned if it didn't make a guy think of sex. The hot, sweaty kind men fantasize about.

"You running shit?" the sailor asked gruffly.

"No. Nothing illegal. We just have to get somewhere quick and on the quiet."

"How quiet?"

"A thousand bucks cash now and a thousand more when we get to Vancouver. And I'll pay all expenses along the way, including fuel."

The guy's eyes opened wide. "You two running from the law?"

Misty shrugged. "No questions or no deal."

The guy nodded readily. "How soon you wanna leave?"

"Five minutes ago."

"Welcome aboard. You'll be wanting to ride below deck, I assume."

Misty flashed him a Marilyn Monroe smile. "Good assumption."

Greg followed her aboard, clenching his jaw at the way the young captain was ogling her. He understood the necessity for her to work the kid over that way. They had no time to play it any other way, but he still didn't like it. An unfamiliar feeling tightened in his gut. *Possessiveness.* Good Lord, where had that come from? He didn't get possessive of women. Particularly ones he barely knew and didn't entirely trust.

They stowed themselves and their gear in the cramped living/sleeping area below while their captain fired up the engines and got ready to cast off. A thick, oily smell of diesel fuel pervaded the space.

Misty muttered, "His engines need a tune-up."

"Do you know how to do it?" he asked in surprise.

"Sure. Don't all girls know how to work on diesel engines?"

He grinned. "The ones worth knowing do."

"We might as well catch a nap. No sense being seen on deck during daylight."

Greg nodded and stretched out on the double bed, rubbing his thigh. "Are you ready to talk now?"

"How about I take a look at your leg first? You've been pretty rough on it today."

His brows shot up. "Are you an EMT, too?"

"Let's just say I've got some first aid training."

"And that list of questions just keeps on growing."

She grinned. "Take off your pants."

"I love it when a beautiful woman says that to me."

She rolled her eyes. "Here. I'll turn my back and you can cover up with this blanket."

While he stripped off his pants, she dug out the first aid kit she'd swiped from the police jeep and pulled out anti-biotic cream, rayon, gauze and a self-adhesive wrap. The mattress rocked as he maneuvered, and then he said, "All right, you can look now. My modesty is protected."

She turned around. "Uh-huh. Just as I thought. Your wound's been bleeding. I knew that dive you took in the electronics store was going to be a problem. Bend your leg."

He propped his foot flat on the bed with his knee sticking up in the air. She reached for the heavy bandages swathing his thigh and unwrapped the wound. The flesh around the puncture wound was red, but not swollen or angry-looking.

She announced, "It doesn't look infected. How deep was the bullet?"

"They said it penetrated at a shallow angle for about ten centimeters. It was about four centimeters under the skin when they dug it out."

Not quite two inches. Deep, but not dangerous as long

as no major arteries had been hit. If one had been, he would've bled to death long before he reached Alaska. He'd been very lucky. The incision the surgeons had made to retrieve the bullet was neatly stitched and intact.

"You didn't tear your stitches. It's just the entry wound that's seeping. When we get somewhere civilized, you'll need to soak that puncture. We need to keep it clean and open until it heals from the inside out."

"That's exactly what the doctor said."

"For now, I'm going to pour some peroxide into it. Since the wound has already been cleaned, this shouldn't sting too terribly. But feel free to take my name in vain."

He had to grit his teeth for all he was worth, but he managed not to make a single sound while she cleaned the wound. She went white around the mouth as though she shared his pain, but did the job with quick efficiency. She covered the wound with antibiotic cream and rayon to keep gauze from sticking to the wound, and then wrapped the whole in gauze and the stretch bandage.

He tried hard not to notice the way her hands slid across his upper thigh, dangerously near parts of him that needed no such attention. But he was only human. He wanted more of her satin-smooth touch upon him. A lot more. He breathed a long sigh of relief when she finally finished.

"Thanks," he mumbled.

She glanced up at him. Their gazes met and held. Awareness shot between them—man-woman, mutual-attraction, relationship-moving-into-new-territory awareness. "You're welcome," she murmured back.

If he didn't distract himself in a big way, and soon, he was going to reach out, drag her down to the bed with him and have his way with her. In more than a little desperation, he said, "Are you ready to talk now? I have some questions for you, too."

Her gaze clouded over. Clearly, she had secrets of her own she wasn't eager for him to probe. He knew the feeling. He was reluctant to ruin the fragile trust they'd built between them. Maybe they should wait a little while longer to have that Talk.

It was stupid to let his attraction to a woman dictate his actions, but they had time. After all, it would take nearly two days to make the run down the Inner Passage to Vancouver. Why ruin the pleasant sense of camaraderie they had right now? It helped stave off the heavy loneliness threatening him.

For the moment, he was content to enjoy her company. It wasn't often he found himself actually taking pleasure in being around a woman. Now that he thought about it, he did spend most of his social time fending off drooling, annoying females. He'd had to deal with it for so long he almost didn't notice it any more. But Misty Cordell neither drooled nor was annoying. In fact, she was as non-needy and self-possessed as any woman he'd ever met.

"Why don't you lie down and take a rest?" he murmured. "You didn't sleep much last night."

"How do you know that?"

He grinned. "You yanked and squirmed at the end of those handcuffs all night."

"Sorry."

"Make it up to me. Keep me warm now." He scooted over and held the blanket up for her.

Doubt flickered across her face, her thoughts completely transparent for once. *Narrow double bed. Occupied by a sexy spy.* Poor baby. She sighed.

He grinned. "It's me or the floor."

"Hmm. Tough choice."

"C'mon. Live dangerously."

That made her laugh. "You have no idea."

No idea of what? But then she crawled in beside him and all logical thought flew out of his head. Suddenly, he felt a distinct urge to drool.

Hal Wittenauer exhaled slowly, hanging on to his temper carefully. "Then who *do* I need to talk to in order to get a straight answer about this operation?"

He was bogged down in middle managers, and nobody at Langley wanted to talk. If the CIA boys and girls didn't get their acts together pretty quick, he was going to call the National Security Advisor and let the shit roll *down*hill until he got some answers.

"I'll transfer you," the bland voice said emotionlessly.

He waited impatiently while he was connected through.

"Agent Whitlock," a strawberries-and-cream female voice drawled in his ear.

Thank God. A woman. Maybe he'd get something done now. After the past year working with the Medusas, he was becoming a born-again fan of professional women.

"This is Hal Wittenauer. I work with the Joint Special Operations Command."

"What can I do for you, General?"

Score one for her. She knew who he was. "I need to talk to the officer in charge of the recent business at Camp Green."

"Ahh. That operation has been designated Vodka Foxtrot."

Hey. A name. That was progress. "Who's in charge of it?"

"I am."

"Outstanding. One of my troops is involved."

"Captain Cordell, I assume. Interesting woman. I have her dossier in front of me."

"I just got off the phone with her."

"Really? What did she have to say?" He could all but see Ms. Whitlock perking up at her desk in interest.

"She said one of your boys tried to kill her and the Russian pilot a couple hours ago."

Silence from the other end of the line. He asked, "Have you sanctioned Nemorov?"

"I'm not at liberty to discuss that."

His eyebrows slammed together. He was not about to stand for bullshit from the operation commander. Nobody shot at one of his girls without a damn good reason for doing so. And he wanted to know what that reason was.

"Fine. Then you can just listen. My operator is as good as they come. She has her orders from your boys. She's to find out what the deal is with Nemorov. But to do her job, she's requesting that you folks back off and give her a little breathing space to work him over."

"And what has she learned about Mr. Nemorov to date?" Ms. Whitlock asked coolly.

"She wasn't in a position to talk freely when I called her."

"I bet she wasn't."

What the hell did that mean? He didn't miss the snide undertone in the Whitlock woman's voice.

Ms. Whitlock continued, "Is your operative a trained interrogator?"

"As a matter of fact, she is."

"And is she trained in methods of psychological warfare?"

He snorted. "She knows more about mind games than you've ever imagined, Ms. Whitlock. You have no idea what Captain Cordell went through to become the operative she is today."

"Tell me, General. Did you meet Mr. Nemorov in person before he fled?"

"No. Why?"

"Ahh."

She didn't say any more. "Ahh, what?" he demanded.

"Then you have no idea of his…effect…on women."

Wittenauer frowned. "What are you talking about?"

"Let's just say he has a rather hypnotic effect on most females."

"What the hell does that have to do with anything? Captain Cordell is a professional. She can separate her attraction to some man from her work!"

"Is that why she was run out of the air force for having an affair with a general officer?"

Wittenauer's temper slipped several notches. "In the first place, those accusations were made by said general's about-to-be ex-wife in the heat of an ugly divorce. No evidence to support the woman's claims was ever found and Captain Cordell steadfastly denied ever being involved with the guy. In the second place, that incident was expunged from Captain Cordell's records when she reactivated her commission to join the Medusa Project. And in the third place, I personally resent your implication. I stand by Captain Cordell's professional decorum one hundred and ten percent."

"I have personal knowledge of the gentleman in question, and he is devastating to women."

Wittenauer barely managed to bite back a snappy comeback about whether or not she'd succumbed to the guy's charms. "So you're suggesting that this ladies' man has turned my Special Forces operative's head?"

"More or less."

"With all due respect, Ms. Whitlock, you're full of shit."

A long silence met that pronouncement.

"Who's your boss?" he asked briskly.

"There's no need to go over my head on this."

"Here's the deal. Cough up the name of your boss, or I'm calling the National Security Advisor and working my way *down* the chain to your boss."

Another long silence.

"I'll patch you through."

"Before you do, Ms. Whitlock—tell your boys to back off. And know this. If your boys shoot at my girl again, I'm putting her under orders to go full offensive. To eliminate everyone she deems a threat whether they initiate an attack on her or not. Do I make myself clear?"

The line clicked and went dead. He'd take that as a yes.

Before he called the National Security Advisor, which he was damn well going to do, he had one other call to make. He pushed the intercom button to his secretary. "Mary, could you do me a favor?"

"Of course, sir."

"Call the Medusas. Tell them Captain Cordell is in trouble and needs back-up. I need whoever among them is medically cleared for field ops to meet me in Seattle. You'll have to arrange transportation."

"I'll take care of it right away."

"Thanks. Now, ring me through to the National Security Advisor."

A dark cocoon cupped Misty, swaying like a hammock in a gentle zephyr of breeze. She inhaled the salty, beloved scent of the ocean. Home. The smell always sent her thoughts dancing back to the beach house. To her childhood. And safety.

"Are you awake?" a male voice murmured in her ear. *In Russian.*

She jolted to full consciousness. She was bloody well awake now. "What time is it?"

"A little after ten."

A glance at the darkness outside confirmed he meant 10:00 p.m. "I slept for six hours?"

"Plus or minus."

"How about you? Did you get some rest?"

"Mm-hm. I've only been awake a little while."

The rise and fall of his voice was soothing. Seductive. Tempted her to relax into it like easy, morning-after pillow talk. "Where's our intrepid captain?"

"In the wheelhouse. Chain-smoking and thinking up ways to blow the money you promised him. Do you have that kind of cash on you, by the way?"

She rolled onto her back. And realized his arm was stretched underneath her pillow and that now her left side was plastered against his from shoulder to knee. She looked up at him from a range of approximately eight inches. "It so happens I do have that kind of cash. I just got back from overseas and I converted all my various currencies into U.S. dollars." *Not to mention the Medusas routinely stash large amounts of cash on themselves for little emergencies just like this.*

"Mmm. Handy."

His tone was just skeptical enough to register that he didn't buy her explanation, but not so accusatory that it demanded the truth. And the tango between them continued.

"Hungry?" he murmured.

She did a quick gut check. "A little. But I doubt Captain Nemo has much of a supply laid in. We didn't exactly give him time to provision up. I have some snacks in my bag." The energy bars she had were no ordinary granola bars. They each packed close to two thousand calories. She could go all day on one if she had to.

He shifted, moving away, and she suddenly craved that warmth all the way down her side. She sat up and swung her feet over the side of the berth. *Distance between them was a good thing. A professional thing. Even if it was only a few inches.*

"So how is it I'm traveling with the female equivalent of Daniel Boone?"

"Hey!" she protested. "I've never worn a coonskin hat! And I've never even been to Tennessee."

"Okay, then. How about the female equivalent of Rambo?"

"Much better." She paused, then asked lightly, "And how exactly is it that a Russian military pilot knows who Rambo is?"

He laughed easily. "Touché."

"Tell you what," she said. "I'll answer your question if you'll tell me your real name."

He considered her for a moment. "Fair enough. You first."

"One more condition. You must never reveal to anyone what I tell you." She smiled, aware the expression didn't reach her eyes. "Or I'll have to kill you. For real."

In a round shaft of amber light cast by the vessel's running lights through a porthole, his eyebrows shot straight up. "Will you make the same promise regarding my name?"

The CIA already knew his name. It wasn't like they needed her to tell it to them. "All right," she answered evenly. "I am, in fact, a pilot in the United States Air Force. However, I also work with a Special Forces team."

"Were you sent to Alaska to kidnap me?" he burst out in alarm.

"Nobody had any idea you were coming. I couldn't have been sent to Camp Green to wait for you. Somebody would have had to know you were coming well in advance and have carefully orchestrated maneuvering me into being up there at the exact right moment. It's not possible."

But as the words came out of her mouth, a dreadful possibility occurred to her. It wasn't entirely *im*possible, either. Various alarming scenarios spun through her brain. "Right?"

He didn't answer.

"Right?" she repeated a little more forcefully.

"My real name is Greg. Gregorii Milovich Harkov."

Chapter 6

Misty was thunderstruck. *Gregorii Milovich Harkov?* He was *Russian?* What in the hell had happened to Greg Mitchell, American? Why had the CIA agents identified him incorrectly to her? Was he even one of their agents? She blurted, "Where were you born?"

"Leningrad. It's called St. Petersburg now, of course."

Was this just another layer of his cover? *Or was that ring of truth she heard in his voice real?* "How did you come to be known as Vasily Nemorov, then?"

"That's three questions, and I only agreed to answer one."

"So ask me two more and we'll be even."

He grinned. "Okay. Who were you talking to on the phone earlier?"

"My boss. General Hal Wittenauer."

"What did you two discuss while you were busy giving him all those yes-no answers?"

"He wanted to know if I was with you and if I knew anything about that dead guy at the camp infirmary. And you heard me tell him about the attack on us in Anchorage."

"What can you tell me about the CIA man in Anchorage?"

"Ahh, ahh, ahh. That's a fourth question for you. You still haven't answered my third one. How did you come to be known as Vasily Nemorov?"

He shook his head. "Sorry. That's classified. I can't go there."

She sighed. "Clearly, neither one of us is in the business of trusting people we've just met. And I can respect that. Heck, it's how I normally operate. But we find ourselves in an extraordinary situation, here. Someone, perhaps more than one someone, is trying to kill you. And I find myself caught in the crossfire. I've shot not one, but two, people on your behalf so far. At what point are we going to abandon our usual caution and start trusting each other?"

He climbed out of the bunk awkwardly, bumping his injured leg in the process and swearing. He went over to the microscopic galley and searched the cupboards. He pulled out a can of soda he found and turned around to face her, leaning his hip against the kitchen counter/map table.

He popped the can open with an aluminum snick and a sizzle of fizz. "Thank you."

"For what?"

"For shooting those guys for me."

"You're welcome." Yet again, he'd turned the subject away from the topic at hand as soon as it got uncomfortable for him. He was really good at that.

He took a sip of soda. "And how is it you casually

shoot two guys and don't show the slightest concern over it?"

"I told you. I'm part of an American Special Forces team. It's what we do."

The can stopped abruptly, halfway to his mouth. "I thought you meant you work with a team. You know, something like…uhh…logistic support. Or…uhh… translating for them."

She studied him narrowly. And accused, "You thought I was a sparrow attached to a male team."

It was too dark to see if he reddened at all, but the expression that momentarily flitted across his face was guilty as hell. *Uh-huh.* That's what she thought. "I already told you. I'm not a sparrow. I'm a Special Forces operator. You know, a soldier. I shoot things and blow stuff up."

It wasn't too dark to see him stare at her. "You're kidding."

'Nope. I'm telling you the God's honest truth. Do you need me to field strip an MP-4 rifle or jerry-rig an improvised explosive device to convince you?" She added dryly, "Usually, killing a couple of hostiles is proof enough of my credentials."

He swore softly, still in Russian. Which reminded her. She asked, "If you're Russian born and bred, where did you learn to speak English so well? And don't lie to me," she added. "You did exactly what I told you to when I yelled at you in English back at that electronics store. And all pilots have to speak English on the radios."

He shrugged, pointedly not switching to English to answer her. Which was probably just as well. Who knew how much of this conversation their captain could hear. "I spent some time in the United States."

"You did more than that. I heard you yell at that lady in

the store in English. Your accent and inflection were beyond perfect. They were native. And your teeth give you away."

"My teeth?"

That startled him. She replied firmly, "Yes. You've had braces. American kids routinely get them and Russian kids all but never get them."

"My mother was American."

"Was?"

"Yeah. She died of thyroid cancer a while back. She was an engineer. She got sent to Chernobyl when the reactor melted down. She was part of the team that figured out how to build the sarcophagus around the site. Some people have a greater sensitivity to radiation than others, you know. She only lasted about five years."

"I'm sorry," she murmured with genuine regret. Although, a little voice in the back of her head whispered that it was a great cover story. Guaranteed to derail any interrogator with the tragedy of his loss. Anyone who knew anything about the sad history of Chernobyl and the thousands of heroic men and women who died trying to save millions of people around the world from the effects of a total meltdown couldn't help but be affected by the reference.

He shrugged. "She died for a good cause. She was okay with it."

"And you? Are you okay with it?"

Another shrug. "I was already cynical about governments in general. The accident didn't do much to alter my opinions one way or another."

Governments, plural. She decided to call him on it. "What governments in particular are you referring to?"

He took a slow drink of soda before answering her. "It's

hard to live outside the U.S. for any period of time and not become cynical about the American government. And it's hard to live inside Russia for any period of time and not become cynical about its government."

He looked as if he'd relaxed some. They had a good flow of dialogue going between them. What the heck. She gave voice to the big, obvious question. "And which government do you serve?"

He drew back sharply. Spilled soda down his shirt. He batted at the beaded droplets and cursed again. She waited out the little performance. When he looked up again, she was still staring at him expectantly. Waiting.

"Well now," he said softly in perfect English. "That would be the $64,000 question, wouldn't it?"

General Wittenauer rose halfway out of his chair in shock. "What the hell do you mean, my operative killed a CIA agent?"

The CIA director's voice crackled over the secure phone line. "You heard me, Hal. My field officer's dead and every witness at the scene says your girl did it. And now she's dropped off the map, gone into hiding."

Wittenauer's mind raced. Why didn't Misty mention that little detail when she was on the phone with him earlier? Was it because the Russian had been there with her? But she'd freely admitted to killing the fake nurse in the same call. Why admit to one killing but not the other? She claimed self-defense in the first killing. Was she trying to buy herself time to flee before the authorities came after her for the second one? The Medusas had no authority to operate on American soil. The first killing had clearly been self-defense and there'd been ample evidence to prove it.

But in the second killing, what she'd done, unless a very narrow set of circumstances were met, was a crime.

Murder, to be precise.

Maybe she didn't know she'd killed the CIA agent in Anchorage. She'd said the guy shot at her and the Russian. That implied she'd shot back, rather than initiated the gunfight. Then she and the Russian had fled the scene. Maybe she hadn't stuck around long enough to realize she'd killed the CIA man.

Into the phone, he said belatedly, "If she shot a CIA agent, she had a damned good reason for doing so."

"Like what?" the CIA director demanded aggressively.

Wittenauer couldn't blame the guy. If one of his troops had been killed by a fellow American, he'd be screaming and hollering for answers, too.

"I haven't gotten a full report from Captain Cordell yet. When I do, you'll be the first to hear about it."

The CIA director was not mollified. "I'm having the FBI put out an APB on her. I want her caught and brought in. Now. And I damned well want to hear her explanation for gunning down a man from the home team in cold blood. He had a wife and kids, dammit."

Wittenauer winced. "I'm certain she didn't gun anyone down in cold blood. That's not her style. I'll do what I can to help you locate her as soon as possible, though. I also would like to have a little talk with her."

He hung up the phone. He had a bad feeling about this. Something was going on at the CIA, and Misty was caught in the middle of it. And he had no illusions about the boys in Langley. If they had a choice between hanging one of their own out to dry or making a sacrificial lamb out of some other poor sod from another government agency, it was a no-brainer which they'd choose. Misty was in big trouble.

He glanced at his watch as he picked up the phone. It would be late evening where he was calling. He dialed a number into the secure phone.

"Go ahead," a male voice said.

Jack Scatalone. The Medusa's primary trainer and direct supervisor.

"Jack. It's Hal. Is Vanessa nearby?"

"Yeah. Why?"

"I need to talk to her."

"Is this official business?"

"Not yet. But I'm afraid it's about to be."

"Just a sec."

A familiar female voice came on the line. "Hello, sir. What's up?" *Vanessa Blake. Team leader of the Medusas.*

"Where are you?"

"At the main house. Everybody's packing. We're flying out tomorrow afternoon to join you in Seattle."

"Tell everyone to be ready to go in two hours. I'll have a private jet pick you up."

Silence met that announcement while Vanessa absorbed the implications of it. "How much trouble is she in?"

"She may have murdered a CIA agent on American soil. Or she may be in the middle of being set up by the CIA."

More silence. Then, "I'm not sure which is worse, but either way, she's in big trouble, isn't she, sir?"

"Get here as quickly as you can, Viper."

"I will, sir. We all will."

Misty stared at Greg—*Gregorii*—in the dark. In Russian, she replied rapidly, "We'd better stick to this language. Less chance of wagging ears understanding."

Her companion nodded and switched back to Russian effortlessly. "Good point. Anything else you want to ask about while we're having true confessions?"

"What's so important about that half-charred box you're all hepped up to recharge?"

He weighed his answer just a moment too long. Whatever came out of his mouth next was going to be a lie—or at least not the whole truth.

"It's a computer with some extremely sensitive data stored on it. Data that I'd like to retrieve."

"Data someone else doesn't want you to have?"

"Correct."

"Who doesn't want you to have whatever's on that computer's hard drive?"

"Several potentially dangerous entities."

"Like who?"

He shook his head at that one. She tried again. "Does the CIA want the information on the computer, or do they simply want to stop someone else from getting it?"

"Ahh. A perceptive question. And one to which I do not know the answer. Their man shooting at us in Anchorage was a surprise to me."

"Why?"

"Why would they shoot at me before they could debrief me and find out what I know and what was on my computer?"

Good point. Why indeed? It made her head hurt to think about the various possibilities that question raised. "You've got to help me out here. I'm getting lost in all the who wants to kill you's and who wants to save you's. Who do you think wants to kill you?"

"I expect the Russian government very much wants to kill me. They don't generally take well to secret aircraft being stolen and flown to America. Apparently, the CIA wants to kill me as well. Although why, I have no idea. I suspect the Russian mafia would like to kill me, but that probably has nothing to do with my fleeing Russia with a prototype MiG and my little computer of wonders. I declined to do a job for them recently, and they don't take no for an answer very well."

She schooled her eyebrows to stay home and not shoot up in response to that revealing comment. A little computer of wonders, huh? Now what did that mean?

"How soon does your computer's battery need to be recharged?"

He glanced at his watch. "We have about twenty hours left."

"We should reach Ketchikan in ten hours or so. Do you want to put ashore before then and get to a reliable electrical outlet, or are you willing to chance it with the boat's generator?"

"I'd rather go ashore. I've gone to a lot of trouble to get this beauty out of Russia with all its secrets. I don't want to take chances with a power fluctuation activating the self-destruct mechanism."

With all its secrets, huh? Yet another interesting choice of words. She asked curiously, "If you had to choose between getting away with the MiG or with this computer, which one would you pick?"

He snorted. "The computer."

Her eyebrows completely got away from her at that one. "Do tell."

"I highly doubt Russia has thought up anything in that jet that the U.S. hasn't already designed *and* counter-acted."

"And the computer?"

"And the computer has information in it that could be valuable for a very long time to come."

"Like what?"

At least he had the grace to look a little regretful when he shrugged and didn't answer.

"We've got company," a voice called down from above in English.

Both Misty and Greg looked up in surprise. She'd almost forgotten they were on a boat. As one, they moved over to the starboard side portholes to have a look. Misty noticed that, like her, Greg stood well back from the round window. No need to put a white, oval, human face in plain view like that.

What looked like another sport-fishing boat was drawing near. The vessel was pristine and white, all neat and tidy. Misty muttered, "I bet they don't catch a single fish on that thing. It might get something dirty."

Greg grinned over at her. "Gee. I'd have guessed that type of boat would be just your taste, all ladylike and perfect."

Is that what he thought of her? That she was ladylike? Perfect? *Huh. Hardly.* He, too, had been taken in by the Barbie-doll exterior. The same tired thought ran through her mind. *She'd never forgive her mother for doing this to her.*

The white boat hailed them with a megaphone to beware of some uncharted iceberg activity up ahead. Apparently, a glacier had calved a huge wall of ice and the entire inner passage was a punchbowl of salt water and icebergs. Misty breathed a sigh of relief when the other vessel moved on, taking its spotless decks and bright spotlights with it.

"Ma'am," the captain called down. "We ought to think about putting ashore soon. It's late and I need some rest, and you heard the guy. There's a lot of ice up ahead."

Misty trotted up the stairs to the bridge with Greg on

her heels. The three of them crowded the small space. She scanned the instrument panel quickly. Not a bad layout. Not state of the art, but serviceable.

"Does your sonar work?" she asked the sailor.

"Yes, of course."

"Then you can go take a nap. I'll drive for a while. With the sonar gain adjusted properly, we'll have no trouble seeing the ice."

"I ain't messing with ice, lady. I'm not tearing up my boat for no amount of money."

She gazed at him coolly. "My life depends on this boat getting through the ice field safely. Do you think I want to risk disabling your boat or ending up in the water and being forced to call the authorities to come save us?"

"Well, no. But…"

"But nothing. I'll take it slow and easy. I know what I'm doing."

The captain's jaw set stubbornly.

"Fine. Two grand more. Three grand when we arrive at our destination."

The guy's stubbornness wavered.

"Stay up here with me on the bridge for a while. Until you're convinced I know what I'm doing." She added with a coaxing smile, "Please?"

The guy huffed. "Okay. Fine."

Greg commented in Russian, "Do you always get your way when you smile at men like that?"

"Pretty much. Why?"

"You're cheating."

"Hah. I'm merely using the weapons at my disposal to get the job done."

"You're taking advantage of a God-given set of genes to manipulate people."

"Trust me. This face was not God-given."

He must have heard the light bitterness she never could quite keep out of her voice when this subject came up. "I beg your pardon?"

"Long story." She turned her back on him and faced the controls. She rapidly named then all off for the captain.

To the Inuit man, she asked in English, "Are you navigating via GPS or some other means?"

"The GPS is hooked to the autopilot, and I'm backing it up with position checks at nav buoys as we pass them."

She nodded. Sound navigation technique. "Good enough. Are you logging our position checks anywhere?"

"The log book's under here." He showed her a shelf below the instrument panel.

She reached out to fiddle with the sonar system. "Your gain is set to map the bottom of the channel. We're out in the middle of the inner passage and cruise ships pass through here, so we know we won't run aground on anything. If you tilt the signal like this," she demonstrated as she spoke, "and adjust the reception so," another twist of the knobs, "the screen will paint any iceberg large enough to cause this vessel a problem."

Indeed, with the next sweep of the sonar screen refresher, a series of red blobs leaped into view. A straight yellow line indicated their GPS programmed course up the center of the screen.

"Now, we just drive around the big chunks of ice and stay as close as we can to our course. No sweat." She gave the captain another brilliant smile for good measure.

Sheesh. Now Greg had her feeling self-conscious about smiling. He was right. She used flirting and her looks all too often to get her way. It wasn't that she wasn't capable of achieving her ends through reason, intelligence, or

courtesy. It was just faster—and easier—to bat her eyelashes and smile a bit. There was nothing hypocritical
about that, right?

Eventually, the captain relaxed about leaving his
precious boat in her hands and retreated below to take a
nap. The night and the stars and the black chill of the ocean
settled around them.

Greg commented quietly, "Peaceful, isn't it?"

"Mm-hm. Almost as peaceful as the sky."

"Is that why you fly?"

She nodded. "I fly to escape the noise of humanity. It's
just me and a jet and all that nothingness. I'm free. A
soaring bird."

"What in your life do you need to fly away from?"

She shrugged. "My life's pretty good. I love my job. I
love the team I work with. I love to travel. To see and do
new things."

"And yet you feel a pull to escape it all. Why is that?"

She asked lightly, "Since when is your middle name
Sigmund Freud?"

He smiled gently. Intimately. "Sorry. I confess, you're
a fascinating woman. I find myself wanting to know more
about you."

"I could say the same. Tell me more about you." He
opened his mouth to object, but she cut him off. "Harmless
stuff. Like your childhood. What was it like growing up
in Leningrad?"

"It was gray. The weather was gray, the buildings were
gray, the people had gray personalities. And cold. Lord,
that place was frigid. We moved to California when I was
ten and I thought I'd died and gone to heaven."

Misty laughed. "Was your father happy in America?"

"He and my mother loved each other very much. Theirs

was a great romance. The kind people make tragic movies over. He was happy to be with her. But no, he missed Russia."

For some reason, a pang of pain flashed through her at the idea of Greg suffering a great loss like that. "So they ended tragically, then?"

"My dad had heart disease. It's why we came to the States. So he could have quadruple bypass surgery. He lasted a few years, but died when he was forty-four. My mom took me back to Russia to honor him by having his son grow up at least partially Russian. And then she died."

She reached out on impulse and squeezed his hand. "I'm so sorry."

His fingers twined through hers. "Don't be. They're better off together like this."

"You must miss them very much."

He looked stricken for a moment. But he answered relatively calmly, "They knew I loved them and I knew they loved me. It was all right. What about you? Do you get along with your parents?"

He was deflecting her again from something he didn't want to talk about. But, having just probed a personal and painful subject, she let him. She reflected on her own strained relationship with her mother. "My father died when I was six. He was sixty-two when I was born, though. I barely remember him."

"And your mother?"

"She's…complicated."

"Ahh. Like mother, like daughter."

Misty jolted. "I sincerely hope not!"

A blob of red loomed ahead on the sonar, and she made a production of steering around it. Squinting, she made out the silvery hump in the darkness. It wasn't much to look at above the water, but according to the sonar, it was massive below the surface. Just the opposite of her. She was all pretty surface.

"My apologies. I didn't mean to make a lovely lady so somber on a beautiful night."

She smiled over at him, for once not bothered by the reference to her looks. "So, tell me. When we get to Vancouver, where do you need to go?"

"To a post office."

Presumably to pick up a letter or package of some kind, then. Perhaps he mailed something to himself before he defected? Or maybe a co-conspirator mailed something to him so it would be waiting for Greg when he got to North America. At least he hadn't ducked her question this time. They were making progress.

Toward what, she had no idea, but progress, nonetheless.

Wittenauer's phone rang in the wee hours of the morning, dragging him from sleep. "Hello," he answered grumpily.

"This is Captain Takamura. I'm sorry to wake you, sir, but you said to call when I had more information on the Cordell affair."

The JSOC night duty officer. Wittenauer sat up in bed. "What have you got?"

"Some good news and some bad news. The syringe on the dead man contained pentobarbital and lidocaine."

"What's that used for?"

"In overdose amounts, which the amount in the syringe qualified for in relation to an adult male's size and weight, it's used to euthanize animals. Makes the heart stop almost immediately after injection."

"Great! So Sidewinder's kill was a good call." Relief flooded him. "I'm assuming that's the good news. What's the bad news?"

"I got a copy of the preliminary police report from the shooting in Anchorage."

"And?"

"The police found no weapon on the man Misty shot and killed."

"What about in the electronics store? Surely the police recovered bullets from the shots the guy fired at her."

"No, sir. I'm afraid not. There were no bullets. And no one reports hearing any shots fired, other than the two Captain Cordell fired at the victim. The only witness, the store manager, says the front window of the store shattered, and Captain Cordell immediately started firing her weapon."

"The CIA agent could've had a silenced weapon and a partner who sanitized the scene before the police got there," Wittenauer retorted.

"According to the report, no one was reported firing at Captain Cordell first. She appears to have murdered an innocent man."

A lump of lead thunked to the bottom of Wittenauer's stomach. "It's a cover-up. Sidewinder was clear in what she told me. They were fired upon and she returned fire. How did the police explain the shot-out store window?"

"The report says that because of fleeing bystanders and arriving emergency services personnel, the glass was kicked around enough that they can't tell much about how the window broke."

He felt too ill to swear. The CIA was setting up Misty all the way. But why? Were they simply covering up for one of their field agents going rogue, or was there something bigger afoot here? He looked at his watch. He sure as hell wasn't getting back to sleep tonight. The Medusas' plane would be landing in a couple hours anyway.

Between now and then, he had a whole bunch of favors to call in. At least it was almost a civilized hour of the morning across the continent in Ottawa. If he was lucky, the Prime Minister of Canada was an early riser. If not, the PM was about to get a wake-up call.

General Karkarov was just climbing into bed when his aide, Gennady, bustled into the room, out of breath. Karkarov sighed. "Now what?" he snapped.

"Sir, we may have a small problem."

"It's late. There had better *be* a problem, and it had better *not* be small for you to barge in on me like this."

The aide winced but held his ground. *Definitely a crisis, then.* "Well, tell me, Gennady!"

"Anatoly Mityonuk, he's a mid-level State Security man, failed a routine polygraph exam today."

Karkarov's blood pressure shot up alarmingly. He snapped, "And this is a problem why?"

"Because he worked for Vasily Nemorov…uhh, Gregorii Harkov."

The general's heart suddenly felt a fist clench around it. "When this Anatoly fellow was questioned further, he revealed something important?"

"Yes, sir. Harkov took a computer with him when he fled. With files. Lots of files."

"That wasn't part of the deal!" The general surged up out of bed. "Bastard! Liar! Cheat!" He whirled and stalked toward his now-quaking aide. "How much?" he roared. "What sort of information did that filthy son of swine steal?"

"Uhh, we don't know yet. Mityonuk is still being questioned. He said he mailed a password to Nemorov...err, Harkov...in Canada. Vancouver to be precise."

"Get a team on it. The sonofabitch double-crossed me. I want him dead. Now."

Chapter 7

Late the next morning, they pulled into port at Ketchikan. Their boat was in need of gas, and Greg was in need of a reliable electrical outlet. Or rather, his mysterious computer was. Soon.

While the captain bought food and refueled, Misty followed Greg ashore. He led the way down the waterfront to possibly the seediest motel she'd ever seen, a long, low building that didn't even bother displaying a sign out front announcing that it was a place of lodging. But then, she suspected not many customers actually spent the whole night there.

She blushed to the roots of her hair when Greg inquired at the cost of renting a room by the hour, but the proprietor didn't bat an eyelash. In no time, they were installed in a desperately grim room. She skirted wide around the bed, unwilling even to touch it. Greg worked quickly, setting up the variable voltage regulator and universal adaptor.

"Do you need me to unscrew the case?" she asked helpfully.

"Good God, no! The self-destruct mechanism is wired to the screws. They're magnetized, and if they break connection with the case, the acid foam will fire."

Her eyebrows shot up. She'd never *heard* of security measures like that in a computer! She eyed the charred box askance. "Where'd you get that thing, anyway?"

He muttered as he fiddled with the voltage regulator, "The headquarters of the URS."

The Russian intelligence service, huh? And didn't *that* just open up some fascinating possibilities for the contents of the hard drive? Aloud, she asked, "What are you doing with that voltage gadget?"

"American outlets produce 110-volt power, Europeans use mostly 220. This system operates at 157 volts. If someone were to plug it in to a regular electric outlet the self-destruct would be triggered."

"157? That's a strange number."

"A prime number. You'd have to know it specifically to send the right voltage through the system. Portions of the most sensitive Russian government buildings operate on oddball voltages for the same reason. No computer can be taken from them and still work."

She tsked. "Amazing paranoia."

He shrugged. "It is quintessentially Russian to be paranoid."

"Are you that quintessentially Russian?" she asked.

He stopped playing with the voltage regulator's knobs and looked up at her, humor dancing in his sienna gaze. "When people really are trying to kill you, it's not paranoia."

She rolled her eyes, laughing. "What a lame line. You can do better than that."

"That's one of the things I like about you. You'd never let me get away with less than my best, would you?"

His observation stopped her cold. They'd truly stepped beyond professional in their relationship. It was where she'd pushed him to go initially, in hopes of throwing him off balance. She hadn't counted on throwing herself off balance in the process, too. In general, she didn't have much use for men. The guys who came on to her were looking for trophy blondes, never looking past her double-D chest. Men interested in intellect in a woman or traits like loyalty never looked twice at her.

"I'm afraid I don't suffer fools well," she remarked dryly.

He grinned. "Me neither." He turned his attention back to the equipment. "If my informant was wrong about the voltage, we'll hear the acid hissing on the hard drive."

He bent his head to the computer case, and Misty did the same. She did it innocently enough, but suddenly realized she'd put them in prime kissing range. The temptation to turn her head and steal a kiss from him startled her.

He murmured, "Has anyone ever told you that you have beautiful eyes?"

A quick blush heated her cheeks. Her eyes were among the few real things about her. Plastic surgeons had had no hand in creating them. She retorted wryly, "Not too many people make it past my chest to my eyes."

His mouth curved into a smile. "You have a great body, too. Great hair, great legs, great smile. But none of that is worth a thing if the soul shining out of the eyes is not kind and generous."

Her heart fluttered. Honest to goodness fluttered. She

had a vision of a smoky jazz club, a wailing saxophone and herself swaying slow and easy in his arms.

His pupils dilated until his eyes were as black as the long winter nights of his homeland. They called to her. The two of them would make magic together if she gave herself over to him....

"Careful," she murmured. "The Russian within you is showing."

His voice was a low caress. "Is that so bad? We Russians are romantics at heart."

She smiled softly. "In a tragic sort of way. You people go for Romeo and Juliet, not Cinderella. No happy endings for you, no sir."

His mouth curved up, pure seduction. "It comes from living in a northern climate. Summer is short and then everything dies."

She couldn't help laughing. "Like I said. Morbid sensibilities."

"Ahh, but the summer is glorious while it lasts."

Sexual energy poured off of him. In buckets. He wasn't offering her anything permanent, but it would be spectacular while it lasted. The temptation to take him up on his unspoken offer was strong. After all, her life was nomadic, too. Not suited for permanent relationships. She came and went on missions, never knowing when or where she'd lay her head down next.

But somewhere in the back of her consciousness she knew that she wanted more. She wanted it all. Home and hearth. Sloppy true love forever. She wanted to be someone's reason for living, not a convenience for the moment.

Regretfully, she turned her gaze to the computer. "Time isn't our friend right now. Throw the switch and let's get this puppy charged up."

"We won't have time to fully charge the battery."

"I'm not worried about a full charge. I just want to give it a boost to buy us a couple of days. By the time it needs another charge, I hope we'll have this mess sorted out and you can charge it to your heart's content."

"From your mouth to God's ear," he muttered. "Here goes nothing."

He flipped the switch.

A faint humming noise came from the box, but no acidic hiss. She looked up, smiling. "I think you did it!"

Their gazes met. Deepened. *Uhh, right.* They both jerked, straightening simultaneously, and bumped foreheads. Laughing, they rubbed their heads.

He cleared his throat. "If we leave this plugged in for an hour or so, that should hold the system for another couple of days. As soon as we get to Vancouver I'll pick up the password and download everything I need."

Password. Vancouver. Got it. She reminded herself to come at him with oblique questions that wouldn't arouse any suspicion. To chip away at what he was hiding, bit by bit. She asked lightly, "What are you going to do with the files once you get them?"

He frowned, not so much at her but as if troubled by unspoken thoughts. He answered absently, "Sell them to the highest bidder, I suppose."

Bidders? What in the world was on that hard drive? "Do you have a price tag in mind?"

He shrugged. "Once the auction's in motion, I'll let the market set the price. But I suppose I'll start at a hundred million dollars. That'll weed out everybody but the serious players."

A hundred million—

She managed not to choke. Her voice was even reasonably calm as she said, "What do you plan to do with that kind of money?"

He answered without hesitation. "Disappear. I want to go someplace quiet and live out my life in peace."

Spoken like a true spy. "Will you go someplace tropical? Or maybe someplace with mountains?" She warmed to the topic. "Hmm. Big city or small town? A ranch maybe? Or a penthouse? Or—ooh, I know—a yacht!"

"I do love water. I'd like to live on a beach. It doesn't have to be a tropical island—that's a little cliché for me—but on a shore would be good."

It figured. As soon as she decided she needed to keep her distance from this guy, he went and started having things in common with her. "I've always loved the combination of rocky cliffs and pounding waves."

He grinned. "As in northern California, or as in the Orkney Isles?"

"I just spent a month running around in the Arctic Circle. I'd have to choose the warmer climate and say California. Even if it does have that whole earthquake, tsunami, fall-into-the-Pacific-someday issue."

He laughed. "What were you doing in the Arctic?"

"Training." And because she definitely didn't need him poking any further into what sort of training she'd done, with whom or exactly where, she added, " and let me tell you. It was hell on my tan!"

"Poor jet-set baby. You'll have to hop over to Saint Tropez and refresh your tan."

How—

Could it be—

No way.

She smiled, but behind her brittle cheeks, her mind positively *raced*. Beach houses in northern California?

Jet setting in Saint Tropez? *Had he seen her classified personnel file?* Or was it just extraordinary luck that he made those particular, back-to-back references? Her family owned a mansion on the cliffs of northern California overlooking the ocean, and her mother was at a private resort on the Gulf of Saint Tropez this very moment with her jet-set pals, brushing up on her tan! Misty'd been dragged on more vacations to the French Riviera than she could count.

Could he have seen her dossier?

What in the *hell* was going on, here?

Just who was playing whom?

Hal Wittenauer sat in the back of the stretch limo, watching through its tinted windows as the Gulfstream business jet taxied to a stop at Spokane's regional airport. Fairchild Air Force Base was only a few miles away, but was not a particularly secure facility. Hundreds of students were at the survival school there at any given time. Better here at a quiet municipal airport where the occasional business jet attracted little attention and its passengers even less attention.

The steps folded down quickly and four women filed out—Vanessa Blake, Aleesha Gautier, Isabelle Torres and Katrina Kim—the remaining Medusa team minus Karen Turner, who was still recovering from a near-fatal poisoning and resultant heart attack.

Next came a man—Jack Scatalone. But then, unexpectedly, two more men climbed out of the plane. Startled, Wittenauer identified Michael Somerset—a recently reinstated MI6 agent, and Dex Thorpe—a Delta team leader who'd worked with the Medusas at the Winter Olympics a few months back. Last came a tall, fair man, helping a blond woman nearly as tall as him down the stairs.

Wittenauer grinned broadly. *Hot damn.* It was good to see Karen Turner up and around again. She'd given them all a hell of a scare when she'd collapsed in full cardiac arrest. The docs said she would make a full recovery and there was no long-term damage to her heart. The blond guy must be Anders Larson—the Norwegian Special Forces observer who'd run around with the Medusas the whole time they were in Norway last month. He recalled Jack mentioning something about Karen and Anders having gotten close.

The two of them looked damned close, the way the Norwegian was hovering over her. Wittenauer's gaze narrowed. He was as protective of his snake ladies as if they were his own daughters. Looked like he'd need to have the same little talk with Larson that he'd already had with the other men about doing right by his girls.

The limo door opened and the whole gang piled in with him. Good thing he'd opted for the stretch model. As soon as Anders closed the door behind Karen, the driver pulled away from the plane. A few well-placed phone calls from Wittenauer had taken care of any need for the team to pass through border patrol. The driver had his orders: cruise around Spokane until Wittenauer told him to stop. There weren't any secure briefing facilities available in the area on short notice, so he'd opted for this rolling fortress in which to bring the Medusas up to speed.

After introducing him to the blond man, who was, indeed, Larson, Vanessa Blake acted as the spokesperson for her team. "How's Misty doing?"

"She's okay so far. No murder charges have been filed yet. There's an APB out on her in Alaska. I've been able to convince the Canadian authorities not to follow suit for now. If she can make it into Canada, it'll buy us a little extra time to sort out this mess."

Vanessa looked grim. "And what exactly is the mess?"

Wittenauer brought her and the others up to speed. He had no qualms about discussing classified information in front of any of the men. All of them were Special Forces operators of one kind or another and had security clearances similar to the Medusas'.

Vanessa leaned forward at the end of the recitation. "So you're telling us that both the Russian government and the U.S. government have tried to kill this Russian guy and Misty?"

"If Sidewinder's telling the truth, yes."

Vanessa shot back, "She's telling the truth."

Wittenauer sighed heavily. "Look. It doesn't happen often, but it does happen now and then—operators do go bad. The pressure or the work itself gets to them. Greed or plain old bloodlust overtakes them and we lose them."

"Not Misty."

Jack intervened. "General Wittenauer has a point. I've known good men—men I'd trust my life to—who've gone off the reservation."

Vanessa glared mutinously back and forth between her new husband and her boss.

Karen leaned forward. "When the drugs had a hold of me, I nearly killed Jack. But I hadn't turned. I don't think we should judge Misty guilty of anything until we have a chance to hear her story. I find it utterly impossible to believe that she'd lose it."

The other women chimed in, voicing their agreement.

Wittenauer sighed. "For what it's worth, I agree with all of you. I don't see her going bad. But in the name of fairness, I had to bring up the possibility."

Vanessa retorted. "Okay, so you've done your job and

brought it up. Now let's discard the idea as absurd and get back to business. What can we do to help Misty?"

"Find her. Get her into Canada. Protect her and the Russian pilot. And help her find out who in hell this guy is and what he's gotten her into."

Crisp nods all around. Not that he'd doubted for a second that the Medusas would take this mission. He was a little surprised that the men wanted in on the action, too. But then, the Medusas had a way of getting under a person's skin. They never failed to earn the grudging respect of their male peers if given half a chance. Vanessa had picked herself a great team, and Jack had done a hell of a job training them.

"In case I haven't told you ladies in a while, it's a pleasure to work with you."

They all smiled warmly back at him. "Likewise, sir," Vanessa answered affectionately. "Now. Where was Sidewinder's last known position?"

"Headed southeast out of Anchorage in a stolen SUV."

"Destination?"

"Unknown. Logically, I have to think they're heading for the lower forty-eight states."

Aleesha looked over at Vanessa. "You think the most like Misty. You're in a stolen car, trying to get to Spokane or places south. What would you do?"

"I sure as heck wouldn't stay on the road for long in that stolen vehicle. I'd dump it and get myself alternative transportation. Problem is, there's only one major highway down the Pacific coast from Alaska to Seattle. Maybe I'd head for the back roads and pick my way south through British Columbia, but that would turn a two-day trip into a four- or five-day trip, minimum."

Isabelle commented, "People are trying to kill Misty and

the guy she's with, and they're on the run from the police. They're in a hurry if she stole a car. They want to get to their final destination and get everything straightened out ASAP."

Vanessa nodded. "So she doesn't go cross-country on back roads. What about flying? Misty could rent a plane and head south that way."

Wittenauer intervened. "I spent most of last night on the phone. I convinced the FAA to review the radar records of every station within several hundred miles of Anchorage. I got the FBI and the Royal Canadian Mounted Police to identify all small aircraft that have taken off in the past twenty-four hours. They've accounted for every last plane. And let me tell you, that was a big job. But Misty definitely did not fly out of Alaska."

Vanessa nodded. "Actually, that makes sense. She's a pilot. People would expect her to fly. She'll do something else." She paused, thinking. "A boat maybe. I'd hire a small private vessel and go offshore into international waters to make a run down the coast. I'd put ashore not far from my final destination. Vancouver or Seattle, maybe. Or maybe someplace farther south in Oregon or California. Depends on what the Russian's trying to do."

Wittenauer nodded. "Makes sense. So. What resources do you need from me?"

Vanessa didn't hesitate. "A fast boat for starters. Vehicles when we put ashore. Weapons. Standard team radio gear. Satellite uplink GPS, time on the NSA observation satellites..."

Misty emerged from the shower rosy and overheated. Thankfully, Greg was trapped beside the computer in the other room, babysitting it as its battery recharged, so she didn't have to leap into her clothes at warp speed.

She hadn't found any answers in the shower. She had

decided she wasn't overreacting, though. To have made two references in quick succession to pieces of data from her classified file was almost certainly not a coincidence. Why did she have to be so bloody attracted to a man she couldn't trust?

With a sigh, she donned her lone set of civilian clothes again. At least she hadn't been running up and down any mountains getting sweaty and muddy in these. Still, when she got a chance, clean clothes would be nice.

She stepped out into the main room. "How's your baby coming?"

"So far, so good. We ought to be able to get out of here in another half hour or so."

"What *ever* will we do to entertain ourselves for that long?"

He looked up quickly, but then quipped back, "You can watch TV and see if we've made the news. I'm going to follow your lead and take a shower."

She waved a nonchalant hand and replied breezily, "All that matters to me is making the society pages."

He snorted with laughter. "Yeah, right. In your line of work, all publicity is bad."

"And it's *not* in yours?" she retorted.

"Yank the plug out of the wall if the computer makes any funny noises or any lights start to blink."

She laughed. "As if pulling the plug will do any good once the computer goes postal. You just want me to sit here and stare at this box?"

"I want you to stay out of trouble." He added almost reluctantly, "I want you to be here when I come out."

Her gaze jerked to his. "I'll be here."

"Promise?"

"Cross my heart and hope to die."

"A simple yes would have sufficed."

She stuck her tongue out at him. "Go take your shower. And I hope I used all the hot water."

Laughing, he retreated into the bathroom.

She tried the television. Nothing but regular programming, and the all-news channels were only covering international stories. Maybe they'd lucked out and avoided making the news at noon. The water in the bathroom had been off for several minutes, and she was still staring at the computer charging when a knock sounded on the door. Misty jerked. They'd rented the room for two hours, and they'd been here only a little over one. Who would interrupt them like this?

"Police. Open up."

Crap.

The bathroom door opened and Greg glided out fast and silent—fully dressed, thankfully. He nodded once. He'd heard.

The two of them looked around for escape routes. There was only the exterior door, a window beside it, and a locked door adjoining the next room over. She gestured at him to get the computer while she sprinted for the adjoining door. Thankfully, she'd grabbed her small rucksack of pilfered police supplies when they left the boat, and she had the right gadget for the task at hand. She pulled out the electric lock pick and poked it into the simple lock. In a matter of seconds, the knob turned under her hand.

She swung open the door.

Greg had grabbed the computer, but the sound of a key being pushed into their room's door lock forced him to abandon the voltage regulator. He dived past her into the next room.

Their room's door opened, jerking against the chain lock she'd rather unthinkingly put on the door earlier. Thank God for good habits like locking all the locks. The cop outside threw his shoulder against the door and the chain's screws tore partly out of the wall. She didn't stick around to see more. She pulled the adjoining door shut behind her fast, slowing only to ease it latched in silence. She locked the knob.

"Now what?" Greg whispered.

"Next door." She sprinted to the next adjoining door and unlocked it, too.

Thankfully, she saw that the third room she let them into was on the end of the motel and had an additional side window. After a quick check outside—all clear for the moment—they scrambled out the window. A quick sprint to distance themselves from the motel, and then they slowed to a walk.

"What the hell was that about?" Greg growled under his breath.

"There must be an APB out on us or our faces were broadcast on the news. The motel manager probably recognized us and called the police."

"How are we gonna get back to the boat? We have to pass the motel to get back to the marina."

She looked around. "Creek Street is this way. I have an idea."

She led the way to the historic street, where all the houses were built on stilts over a running salmon creek. It only took a moment to spot what she wanted. A small power boat moored underneath one of the brightly painted houses.

"You're up, Greg. Can you hot-wire a boat?"

"Ignition systems are all pretty much the same."

He lay down to work underneath the vessel's dashboard while she wrapped the computer in a waterproof tarp.

"Give the engine a try," came his muffled voice.

She gave the outboard motor's starter button a poke and the engine sputtered to life with a puff of smoke. Greg cast off and she guided the boat toward the main harbor. "I think I saw a couple of raincoats in that storage bin."

Greg pulled out two yellow slickers and passed her one while he donned the other. She moved over to the right side of the traffic buoys and kept her speed at the posted limit.

Three police cars were parked at oblique angles in front of the motel they'd just vacated, and a fourth pulled up while they were floating past. The word was definitely out on the two of them.

They continued around the point and motored into the marina where they'd left their vessel. Misty said as quietly as she could over the engine noise, "Have a look and make sure our captain hasn't turned us in for whatever reward's being offered."

Greg peered in between the rows of moored boats. "Looks clear."

They moved in cautiously, but there was no help for it. If cops were waiting for them aboard their boat, they'd have to board it to find out. Misty steered into an empty slip a few boats down from theirs. She tied off the boat quickly.

"You take the computer, Misty. That leaves my hands free to fight."

"I hate to burst your bubble, but unless you're a world-class specialist in unarmed combat, you probably ought to be the one carrying the computer so *my* hands are free."

He smiled, unfazed. "If I weren't such a good-looking guy with such a solid self-image, a girl like you could be hell on my self-esteem."

She grinned back at him. "Glad to hear your ego isn't too badly punctured."

"Shall we?"

"Let's."

She climbed out of the little boat first and steadied it as Greg followed, awkwardly hefting the computer. "Give me about a thirty-second head start," she murmured.

"Go get 'em tiger."

She smiled at him and their eyes met, brimming with words not spoken.

Be safe.

I will.

I don't want anything bad to happen to you.

You either.

Oh yeah. They'd gone way past the professional acquaintance stage. She moved quickly toward their boat. No unusual movement on the dock. All the nearby boats looked deserted. No furtive movements of curtains in windows or shadows fading off decks.

Their captain was on the rear deck of their vessel, stowing what looked like a grocery bag of canned goods. He nodded casually as she approached him. Good sign. Showing no undue stress.

"Ready to go?" she murmured as she climbed aboard. The deck rocked lightly beneath her feet.

"Yup. You?"

"Almost. My friend will be here soon." She moved downstairs quickly and cleared the small space. She glided back out on deck and poked her head into the bridge to clear it as well.

"You wanna check the engine compartment to make sure I ain't got no cops stashed down there?"

She turned, surprised, to face the young captain. She

grinned, chagrined. "No, that's all right. Only one or two could fit down there, and I could take that many cops with one arm tied behind my back."

The guy laughed. "Here comes your friend. I'll go start her up if you two wanna cast off."

They were under way in a matter of minutes. Misty breathed a huge sigh of relief when they turned out into the main channel of the Inner Passage a little while later and continued their journey southward.

That had been a close call. Far too close. She needed answers from Greg, and she needed them now. Whether he liked it or not, the time had come for Gregorii Harkov—or whatever his name was—to spill his guts.

But how to get that to happen? He was as cagey as anyone she'd ever met, and after spending the past year around famously close-mouthed special operators, she knew what a challenge she faced.

"I wasn't sure we were going to make it out of there," he commented from beside her, the wind ruffling his short hair into a glamorous tangle.

She nodded. "Yeah, that was close. The last thing I wanted to do was shoot at cops."

"Man, you moved fast to get us out of there. You whipped through those rooms like a sidewinder."

A *sidewinder?*

She went hot all over, then shivered with nausea. *That was her field handle.* How in the *bloody hell* did he know that? No more than a dozen people in the entire world knew that name!

Chapter 8

Greg stared around the tiny cabin of the fishing boat, both refuge and prison cell. That had been a close call back there. Without Misty's quick thinking and extraordinary skills, they'd be in jail right now. Or worse.

What was he doing? This junket had turned into a complete disaster. It had seemed like such a straightforward deal when he'd made it with General Karkarov. Greg—or Vasily as the general knew him—wanted to retire from the spy business, and Karkarov needed a plane flown out of Russia.

Vasily would defect with the prototype MiG and scare the hell out of the American defense community with this evidence that the Russians had mastered high-tech stealth technology. Of course, the MiG was a fake. They'd worked up one plane to look like something radical and new, flown it out, let the Americans get a brief glimpse of it, and then blown it up...right on schedule.

For his part, Vasily could be trusted to keep his silence once he was out of Russia, not only because he'd been a loyal spymaster for decades, but also because the Russians could always reveal that Vasily had been part of a ruse to trick the Americans.

The Russian Intelligence Service never let its people go quietly into the night. And its spymasters certainly were not allowed to retire and move to the United States, into the bosom of the snake itself. Had he tried to flat-out defect, the Russians would have tracked him to the farthest corners of the earth and murdered him, publicly and horribly, as an object lesson to other URS agents never to try the same. Flying out the jet had been the perfect arrangement. Karkarov got what he wanted, and Vasily—in actuality, Greg—got his freedom. Karkarov thought Vasily was making a great sacrifice by leaving Russia, never to return. And Greg got to go home.

But that's where the plan had gone awry. He was supposed to flee to the United States and be welcomed back with open arms by the American government. They were supposed to be tremendously impressed with the intelligence he'd gathered while he was living as Vasily Nemorov, and he'd be a hero within the CIA for his audacious mission.

But instead they'd tried to kill him! They hadn't even waited to talk to him, to ask where he'd been all that time, before they started shooting at him, the bastards. The assassination attempt had thrown an *enormous* monkey wrench into his plans. It had forced him to improvise, and he hated improvising. Once agents started winging a plan, it always went to hell fast. And sure enough, he was in a big mess now.

It wasn't all bad being on the run with a beautiful woman. But if she was lying to him about sincerely wanting to help him, he was in even deeper trouble. The police obviously had an APB out on them, and he had no doubt the CIA was after them with both barrels. Nobody killed a CIA man and lived to tell about it if the agency had anything to say about it.

He'd half expected the Russians to try to kill him. But he'd counted on the CIA's formidable resources to protect him. *Stupid him.*

He had no contacts left who weren't CIA, no money, no safe place to hide. Just a computer full of information that, if he was damned lucky, he might turn into enough resources to hide for a few years from the governments trying to kill him. It was the best he could hope for now.

What he was supposed to do with Misty, he had no idea. He knew what he *wanted* to do with her. Surely he wasn't imagining the vibes between them—the sexual spark that flared up every time they got within three feet of each other. But for all her superficial flirting with him, she had a reserve about her that didn't invite that kind of attention. Held her cards close to the chest, she did.

For now, all he could do was hope he wasn't imagining the heat between them. That, and hope she didn't betray him before he had a chance to explain himself to her, to gain her trust, to make her understand why he wasn't on anybody's side in this chess game any more.

He just wanted some peace and quiet in his life. A chance to find a woman like Misty, a woman who was *real,* and settle down. Raise a family. Live out his days as a normal person. Was that too much to ask?

He refused to wallow in self-pity, dammit.

But that didn't mean he was any less attracted to her.

* * *

Misty paused at the top of the stairs leading down into the living quarters. She couldn't believe she was going to do this. She'd always vowed she'd never use sex as a weapon. But damned if she wasn't about to play the sex kitten with him to make him talk. What choice did she have? She had to know what—*who*—she was up against.

How did he know so much about her? Was Greg the enemy, or was he merely using her for some unrevealed purpose? What was his agenda?

If she was compromised, then the entire Medusa Project was compromised. And she'd do whatever it took—*whatever* it took—to ensure her teammates' safety.

How in the world had someone found out about them? Greg had to have gotten hold of her classified dossier. When the Medusas were formed, they were supposedly erased from the system. No personnel files, no payment records, no FBI files, no security check reports should remain. Everything was supposedly erased. Even their driver's licenses and birth certificates supposedly ceased to exist.

Could someone within the Medusa Project have leaked the information? But who?

No way had one of her teammates done it. They would all die for each other. Their supervisors? Jack Scatalone or General Wittenauer? Impossible. They were both special operators from way back and both men had gone to bat for the snake ladies countless times. There was always the President of the United States. Certainly, holders of that office had been known to throw their subordinates to the wolves before. But this President had been fiercely protective of the secrecy of the Medusa Project to date. It didn't feel right that he'd spill the beans on them.

Someone else, then. For all Misty knew, some admin type in the Department of Defense personnel center could've handed over the Medusas' records to the Russians. In this information age, it was nigh unto impossible actually to keep a secret for any period of time.

She took a deep breath. Right now, the culprit didn't matter. The fact remained that the cat was out of the bag. Greg knew who she was, and she had to assume he knew who all the Medusas were.

She had to warn them.

If she knew Hal Wittenauer, he'd called the other Medusas by now to let them know there was a problem. And if she knew them, they'd be attempting to track her down. To join her. Because that was what she'd have done for any one of them. Her teammates would have their cell phones on, or at least be checking their messages periodically.

She headed for the phone-booth-sized bathroom, locked herself in, and pulled out her cell phone. She dialed Vanessa Blake's number.

It picked up on the second ring. "Go ahead," her friend and team leader said tersely.

"Thank God you're there," Misty murmured. "Can you hear me okay?"

"Sidewinder? Is that you? Where are you?"

"I can't talk for long. I think I'm compromised, which means the Medusas are probably also compromised. You need to stay away from me or we'll all go down."

"What are you talking about?"

"The man I'm with knows who I am. He has to have seen my dossier."

"Who is he?"

"I'm not sure—"

She broke off as a male voice sounded right outside the toilet door. "Misty? Are you in there? Is everything okay?"

Vanessa said urgently, "Go to Canada, Sidewinder. The American police are looking for you. General Wittenauer worked a deal with the Canadians, though—"

Misty groaned through the door panel, "I'm a little seasick. I'm taking pills for it as we speak." She disconnected the phone and stuffed it in her pocket. She flushed the toilet and stepped out onto deck. "How embarrassing is this? The pilot with the supposedly cast-iron stomach getting nauseous?"

He shrugged. "You've been under a lot of stress. That alone can cause stomach upsets."

Indeed it could. She was feeling more than a little of that very stress as they spoke, in fact. "Do you know if there are some crackers on board? Those always work in flight to calm down my gut."

"Let's go check."

She noticed how adroitly he was maneuvering to make sure she wasn't by herself any more. Damn. He must've heard her talking on her cell phone. She said casually, "I was checking my voice mail messages when I got sick. I have a bunch of messages from my boss alternately cajoling and threatening me if I don't bring you in pretty soon."

He looked mightily startled. The content of her boss's messages couldn't be that big a surprise to him. Must not have expected her to 'fess up to being on the phone. But then his eyebrows lowered suspiciously again. Damn. He must've realized you don't talk back to your voice mail.

She added, "I called him back. I left a message saying you and I were driving into Canada for a few days to sort everything out and that I'd be in touch. It's not much of a misdirect, but every little bit helps."

That really sent his eyebrows up. Better, it threw a look of confusion into his gaze. Yup. It was all about keeping him off balance. His suspicions held at bay for the moment, she announced, "Let's go see if we can find those crackers. My stomach still is heaving, and it'll take those motion sickness pills a few minutes to kick in."

He lurched into motion. "Of course."

She followed him toward the living area. Damned if she didn't notice his broad shoulders and easy grace as he moved. She found both incredibly attractive. But they also spelled fitness and agility—and in a foe, those spelled danger.

Could she bring herself to sleep with him—her possible enemy? At least the moment of truth was not yet at hand. Any good fall from grace took time.

First up on the seduction agenda: a good meal. She poked around to see what supplies the captain had laid in. Too bad there weren't a couple of filet mignons and a nice bottle of wine. She made do with whipping together a quiche lorraine. She didn't have a rolling pin to flatten the dough, which she'd improvised from pancake mix, but a girl worked with what she had. She shaved Swiss cheese with a paring knife in lieu of grating it, but she got the bacon, cheese, egg and milk filling right at any rate. She popped her creation into the tiny oven to bake.

Next on the agenda: polish herself to a high Barbie-doll gloss. She brushed out her hair and pulled it back from her face, twisting it up into a sophisticated knot. She didn't have much makeup with her, just a little mascara and lip gloss. Fortunately, she was one of those women who looked nearly as good without makeup as with. Besides, if she laid on the seduction too heavily, Greg would get suspicious. Well, more suspicious than usual.

Last on the agenda: create a romantic atmosphere. She made the bed and straightened up the cabin, and she stuck a bit of candle she found into an empty beer bottle. She set the table and stood back to admire the results.

"Why the home-sweet-home routine?" Greg murmured, practically in her ear.

She jumped. How had he gotten right up behind her like that without her hearing him? Her threat assessment of him climbed another notch.

She murmured, "Normalcy, or even just the appearance of it, can significantly reduce tension and stress in the middle of a tough mission. I figured we were both due for a break."

"You look especially lovely tonight."

She turned—whoa! And found herself chest to chest with him in the confined space. "Thanks for noticing."

"It's hard to be around you and *not* notice."

"Thanks for trying not to notice."

"You're welcome. Remind me not to appreciate beautiful women more often."

His voice was a stroke of silky-smooth sable down her spine, and her tension unfolded fractionally. She waggled a finger at him. "As long as you're with me you'd better not notice other beautiful women."

"Jealous are we?"

"Not in the least. It's just rude to look at other women when you're already with one."

"True." He captured her wagging finger and, dropping a quick kiss on the tip of it, released it before she had time to react.

What was that all about?

He said, "I think your quiche smells ready. I'll open a can of fruit cocktail while you pull it out."

They spent the next few minutes in the tiny galley generally getting into each other's way. Each time she bumped into him, a little more of Misty's tension evaporated. There was no denying her attraction to him. If they'd met randomly somewhere in the real world, she'd have gone after him all the way. And it wasn't just his looks. His humor and intelligence made him that much more attractive.

Greg lit the candle and she sliced and served the quiche. He held her chair while she sat down and then slid into place across from her at the tiny table. It might as well have been a private dining room in a five-star restaurant. The low rumble of the engines and the sound of water rushing by made for relaxing background music. Candlelight might have a reputation for making women look their best, but it did a number on Greg, too. He was breathtakingly handsome in the flickering glow.

They compared their favorite places around the world, listed favorite museums, the best beaches, their taste in music. It was all so very normal, so very *real*. It didn't feel at all like part of the overall cat-and-mouse game between them. And yet, that was exactly what it was. Separating Greg's magnetism and her reaction to it from the mission at hand was harder than finishing the final leg of a triathlon—a full-blown marathon. Nonetheless, that was her job. Time to move into high gear.

"So tell me, Greg. Do you flirt as a matter of habit, or do you mean it?"

"I don't flirt with every woman I meet." He added playfully, "Just the good-looking ones. What about you? Beautiful American blondes have quite a reputation for liking to party."

"Ahh, but you see, I'm not really a beautiful blonde."

"You could fool me."

She said nothing, reflecting for a moment on her past. She looked up in surprise when his hand grasped hers.

He said quietly, "That's not the first time you've said something like that. What do you mean by it? You see the same woman in the mirror that the rest of us do. You must know you're a stunning woman."

She sighed. It wasn't something she talked about. Ever. But then his thumb rubbed across her palm and her insides turned to jelly.

"What puts that sad look in your eyes, *milochka?*" Darling.

He'd just called her his darling. And something needy within her unfolded, grasped for the affection he offered. God, she hadn't realized how lonely she was. Still, his attentions might be every bit as calculated as hers.

"Talk to me," he urged.

She sighed. "I was in a car accident when I was seventeen. A bad one. I had a seatbelt on, but the shoulder harness wasn't adjusted properly. My face hit the dashboard and was pretty much erased."

His fingers tightened around hers.

"All of the major bones in my face were shattered. They had to do a complete facial reconstruction."

"The surgeons did remarkable work."

Bitterness crept into her voice. "When they asked my mother for a picture of me to use as a guide in repairing my face, she refused. She told them to make me pretty. And this is what they did to me."

His fingers crushed hers for a moment, and then released. He said quietly, "Aren't you grateful they didn't make you into a monster?"

"Of course. The surgeons did an amazing job. But don't

you see? I wasn't good enough the way I was. My mother told them to make me prettier."

"Let me guess. She's a beautiful woman."

"An international beauty queen, model and actress."

"Hmm. And your father was much older and very, very rich. She used her looks to land him and assiduously maintained her physical perfection as long as he was alive."

"She still does."

He shrugged. "I feel sorry for your mother."

Misty blinked, surprised. "How's that?"

"Her looks were all she had. The only way she could get what she wanted was to trade on them. You, on the other hand, have so much more going for you than that. If anything, your looks are secondary to your primary attractions."

Okay, if this guy were playing straight with her, she could seriously fall for him. Fast. But it was all part of their *danse dangereuse*...

Not one bit of it was real. And that was the most bitter truth of all.

Vanessa hung up the phone reluctantly. The rest of the team looked at her expectantly. "We need to get to Vancouver. Now. She's on a boat. And she thinks the Medusas have been compromised."

The effect of her words on the others was electric. General Wittenauer started making phone calls. Aleesha leaned forward and knocked on the partition separating them from the driver. "Take us back to the airport," she directed.

Jack got on the phone and told the pilots of the recently landed Gulfstream to fuel up, file a flight plan to Vancouver, and stand by for an immediate departure.

Isabelle and Dex pulled together the supply list, checking off the things they could get when they landed and the things they'd need to pack or procure before departure. The two of them got on the phone to the Spokane SWAT team and the Fast Reaction Strike Team at Fairchild Air Force Base to ask for toys.

Vanessa called the National Security Agency and asked for an immediate trace on Misty's cell phone position. She waited on the line while the search was made.

"I'm sorry, ma'am," came the reply a few minutes later. "That phone is not currently turned on."

"Thanks. Can you keep a search open for that number so the next time it gets turned on you get a fix?"

"That'll take some high-powered muscle to approve—"

"If you'll keep the search active for sixty seconds, I'll have the White House call you within that minute. Is that high enough for you?"

The satellite operator replied dryly, "Works for me."

Vanessa made the call to the White House, then hung up again. *C'mon Misty. Don't be a cowboy and try to handle this alone.* If the Medusas were truly compromised, that was all the more reason for the team to stick together right now. That Russian guy had better not hurt Misty. The protective violence of a mother bear surged through her.

She spent the next hour too busy to do much more worrying.

"Dance with me."

How did he do that? He kept plucking the thoughts right out of her head! She no sooner thought of dancing with Greg than he mentioned it.

He held out his hand to her, and Misty stared at it, mesmerized. His waiting palm dared her to play with a fire that would burn her as surely as it would thrill her beyond imagining. Slowly, she laid her hand in his. How could she not accept? She lived for danger.

He tugged her to her feet and drew her close, wrapping her in his arms. No formal foxtrot, this. No cautious observance of proper distance, no tentative exploration of personal space. This was chest to chest, belly to belly, thigh to thigh, as close to sex as dancing got.

"There isn't any music," she murmured.

"Does it matter?" His lips curved into a smile.

"No." She sighed.

He murmured, "The music we make is limited only by our imagination."

Now why did she get the impression he wasn't talking about music at all?

"What should we dance to? A waltz? Or maybe an alto saxophone wailing the blues? Or should we go ahead and pick out 'our song'?"

"How about, 'From Russia with Love'?"

He laughed. "Perfect."

She replied lightly, "And which character are you? Heroic James Bond saving the world, or the loyal but conflicted Russian agent sent out to seduce James?"

He drew her head to his shoulder and continued to sway with her. *And didn't answer.* What was it going to take to get him to be square with her?

Finally, he murmured, "I'm neither character. I'm not out to save the world. I never was."

"How did you end up in the spy game, then?"

"It was chosen for me."

"By whom? Your parents, or a government?"

He shrugged. "The KGB started using me when I was

too young to tell them to go to hell. And the CIA approached me not long after that. They both paid well and the idea of being James Bond was sexy, so I went along with it."

"So you worked for both sides? A double agent?"

He frowned. "Not a double agent. A freelancer. I never played one side against the other. I never..." A pause. "...chose."

She leaned back to stare up at him. Shock coursed through her. "How can that be? How can you not have chosen one side or the other?"

"It was a delicate dance, indeed. I chose my missions with incredible care."

"And you honestly thought you could keep that up for the long term?"

"I can't say that I gave it any great thought until I was too deeply mired on both sides to extract myself."

"Is that what you're trying to do now? Extract yourself?"

He chuckled quietly. "Certainly not. I'm perfectly content right where I am...wrapped in the arms of a lovely lady."

Damn. Another misdirection!

"Let's not think about any of that tonight," he murmured into her hair on a warm breath. "This evening is about relaxing. Taking a break. This time is just for us."

If only there were an "us." And if only they could create a time and a place just for them. Alas, it was not to be. But then his finger tipped her chin up. In the guttering of the candle, he gazed down at her with passion that warmed her very core.

"I want you."

Whether he'd said the words aloud or not, Misty wasn't certain. And she wasn't sure she cared.

Almost as if it were an unwilling afterthought, he sighed. "I have been alone for so long."

And that was what did her in.

She knew what it was to be alone. And the plea in his voice was more than she could bear.

Waves lapped against the side of the boat, setting the deck rocking ever so slightly under her feet. The fiery atmosphere inside was all the hotter for the sea's cold embrace surrounding them. Everything made her burn. The flickering candlelight. The low rumble of the boat's engines. The night's deep silence beyond.

He was wildfire and she a roaring wind, stoking his inferno, sending it raging out of control even as she drew it into herself. Her hands skimmed across his skin under his sweater. And he burned, more flame than flesh. For her.

His wool sweater floated over his head. And then his magnificent body was bare before her. Craving rushed through her. A need to taste him, to smell him, to feel him, sent her mouth to his skin. She pushed aside a thin chain with a small key hanging from it to taste him. The muscles of his stomach contracted hard beneath her lips, his sharp, indrawn breath drawing a smile from her. His belt slithered free of his lean waist and thudded to the floor. And then he was drawing her up against him, lifting her to meet his kiss.

And the tongues of flame licking at them exploded until the entire boat burned around them. Their shadows danced upon the walls, rising higher and higher in the candle's golden glow, melding into a single, sinuous shape. They turned slowly, riding the steady rocking beneath their feet, their bodies absorbing the rhythm of the sea.

He tasted her with tongue and lips, and she speared her hands into his hair, drawing him closer as she nipped and sucked at him. Who devoured whom, she couldn't say, but to call their mutual inhalation of one another a kiss wasn't nearly adequate.

He made short work of her sweater and pants, baring her skin to the kiss of the candlelight and his questing mouth. He lowered her to the bed almost without her noticing. But she became aware of her hips lifting to his with the sea's naked power, a rhythm more primal than thought, a driving instinct more ancient than time.

And then they were one. He groaned and she shuddered, and they strained toward each other, reaching inside one another's very souls, ripping away all artifice, all restraint, all pretense of anything other than Man and Woman.

And finally, wrung out to the very dregs of their beings, they collapsed. The sea was quiet once more, the storm between them spent. But the veil between them was still torn away, their souls raw and naked to one another.

A single thought pierced her utter physical and emotional exhaustion.

Merciful Mother of God, what had she done?

Chapter 9

Vanessa Blake glanced around the hotel suite. It was crowded with her teammates all working phones and computers, teasing information out of various individuals and agencies to piece together a picture of what had really happened to Misty.

Every hour on the hour since 4:00 p.m., they'd been getting together to compare notes. It was 10:00 p.m. now.

"Time for an update, gang." Everyone looked up and gave her their attention. "Jack got the list of supplies Misty and the Russian bought at the electronics store in Anchorage just before the shooting."

She flashed a list on the wall with her laptop's projector capability. "Any guesses what they were planning to do with this stuff?"

Aleesha, the Medusas' explosives expert piped up. "It's not the right stuff for improvising a bomb. Doesn't look like booby-trap gear either."

Isabelle, their communications guru, added, "It looks more like the sort of stuff I'd use to power up a radio. Or a computer."

"But why a variable voltage regulator?" Vanessa asked.

Isabelle shrugged. "Not all radios or computers run on American 110-volt power. Perhaps they're working on a piece of foreign equipment."

The conversation died. Vanessa moved on to the next piece of information they'd gleaned in the past hour. "Misty and the Russian rented a motel room in Ketchikan for two hours. They probably came in by boat and docked within a couple of blocks' walk of the motel. So they go ashore, rent the room, and do what?"

General Wittenauer looked over at Jack and said solemnly, "Son, haven't you shown your wife what men and women do in motel rooms by the hour?"

A laugh rippled through the team and the wife in question—Vanessa—rolled her eyes. She stated firmly, "Misty's *not* going to stop to fool around with the law on her heels and people trying to kill her. Which brings us back to my original question. Why the motel stop?"

"To shower and clean up?" one of the men suggested.

Vanessa shook her head. "Misty's too much of a pro to risk her life for a bath."

The other Medusas nodded their agreement.

Again, the conversation died, and she moved on. "The motel manager said they checked in a little before noon. He saw their pictures on TV at 12:25 p.m. Apparently he debated what to do for a while and called the police at 12:50 p.m. The police broke into the room at 12:57 p.m. It showed signs of very recent occupancy, but Misty and the Russian were gone."

She flashed up a map of southeastern Alaska, a long,

thin arm of land and islands stretching along the coast of British Columbia.

"They leave Ketchikan soon thereafter, presumably by boat, since Misty called me last night and mentioned being seasick to someone before she hung up the phone. Cruising at an average speed of twenty knots for the past eighteen hours, that puts them nearly back in Anchorage, or four to six hours out of Vancouver."

Jack added grimly, "Assuming they haven't already put ashore somewhere in British Columbia and continued fleeing over land."

She shrugged. "If that's the case, we won't find them until Misty wants to be found. But here's the thing. Why are they heading south by boat? Why not drive north into Denali and lose themselves up there indefinitely? Alaska's a huge place. I have to believe they have a specific destination in mind."

"I'd guess Vancouver or Seattle," Jack replied. "Otherwise, your girl would've grabbed an airplane and flown out. It would take too long to get to a really distant destination over land."

Vanessa nodded. "Logical. Sounds like the way Misty would think. But Vancouver and Seattle are both big cities. We don't stand a chance of searching both with our resources and finding her. And I don't want to call in the authorities unless I absolutely have to."

Aleesha asked wryly, "Anybody got a coin we can toss?"

Vanessa shook her head. "Let's think about this. I told Misty the American authorities are looking for her and to head for Canada. All else being equal, I bet she'll heed my warning and go to Vancouver. Can anyone come up with a better reason for choosing one over the other?"

Silence was her only answer.

"Okay, then. I say we give ourselves a few more hours to turn up some new information. If we don't find anything new, then we pack up this dog-and-pony show and head for Vancouver. We can stake out the docks and watch for incoming boats from the north."

Jack said quietly, "There's a lot of coastline in that area. It'll be a search for a needle in a haystack."

"Yeah, but she's my needle. I want my operator back."

Greg stared up at nothing. A flickering red reflection from the ship's running lights off the surface of the water shined through the porthole, turning the cabin's ceiling into a hellish montage. *What had just happened?* She'd broken through his psychological and emotional defenses as though they were made of tissue paper. He'd taken one look at her in the candlelight, and he'd needed her worse than life itself. Needed to connect with her. To feel the fire within her and become part of it. And he certainly had. They'd burned the night down around them.

And yet, it had solved nothing.

He still had no country to call his own, no place to go that was safe. He had nothing to offer her. No home. No life. *No future.* If he gave half a damn about her, he'd walk away from her. Give her a shot at a real life with someone else. But the thought of letting her go ripped his guts out.

Now what the hell was he supposed to do?

Tomorrow he'd get the password, retrieve the data from the hard drive, and blackmail both the Russians and Americans into leaving him alone. *Alone* being the operative word. It lay bitter on his tongue. But that was tomorrow. They still had tonight.

And right now, he was as sated as a Roman and relishing every inch of Misty's satiny softness snuggled up against him. The woman drove him out of his mind. With sexual need, with intellectual challenge, hell, with laughter.

He didn't even want to think about the danger she'd be in if the people chasing him thought Misty was important to him. They'd kill her so fast it would make his head spin. All to get to him.

Why couldn't they just leave him alone? He didn't want to be part of their jockeying any more! But how did a man who'd been the tool—the weapon—of two powerful and occasionally ruthless governments tell those very regimes to go to hell?

Misty shifted beside him, drawing away fractionally.

Great. And now she was pulling back from him, too.

"Don't go," he murmured.

She subsided against his side. But her tension was palpable. He craned his neck to look down at her. "Are you comfortable?"

"Mm-hm."

"Not too freaked out?"

"Why would I be freaked out?"

"I'm freaked out," he replied candidly.

That had her propping herself up on his chest with her elbows in no time. "Why?" she demanded.

So much for the soft, relaxed version of Misty, practically purring with satisfaction at having lured him out of his debonair disguise.

In a rare moment of complete honesty, he answered, "I wasn't looking for this. For you. You're a complication I don't need right now."

"Why not?"

"I don't want to put you at risk."

"Why am I at risk?"

He smiled his best James Bond smile up at her. "My, you do ask a lot of questions, my dear."

"Look. What happened between us was—" she hesitated.

"Magical? Earth-shattering? Life-changing?"

She exhaled hard. "I was going to say a mistake."

He frowned. It was his turn to fling a question at her. "Why? What was a mistake about this? You know as well as I do we've been attracted to each other from the first moment we laid eyes on each other."

She laughed reluctantly. "I have to admit, I was attracted to your voice on the radio before I ever laid eyes on you."

"And I to yours. It was Fate that brought us together."

"Was it really?" she asked lightly, but with a deadly serious undertone.

"What do you mean by that?"

"I have to ask myself how you managed to make off with a highly classified, prototype aircraft at all. Then you happened to fly into the one place in Alaska likely to have a Russian-speaking American pilot up on the radios at the very time you came streaking over the horizon. And then, you happen to know details about me that no one— *no one*—should know. The coincidence is just too great."

Shock slammed into him like a Russian tank. *She'd figured out his defection had been a setup?* How, for the love of God, had she gotten to that? He ought to deny it. The lie was on his lips. But he could not speak it. Not to her. Not after what they'd shared.

"How did you know about my personal life? My field handle?"

"Your what?"

"The nickname my teammates call me."

"I have no idea what you're talking about."

"Riiight. And I'm supposed to buy that. You just pulled a reference to sidewinders out of thin air."

"Huh? Oh. I've always been fascinated by how they can move over hot sand so quickly, never appearing to head for their intended destination, yet always ending up there."

She stared down at him doubtfully.

She was beyond beautiful in the scant glow from the porthole. If that was a man-made face, the surgeon who had created it was a master. "I don't want to argue with you, Misty. Can't we just relax and savor the moment a little while longer?"

She sat up, dragging the top sheet with her and wrapping it around her as she stood up. He caught a glimpse of the perfection of her body before she swathed it in a makeshift toga.

"No. We can't."

"Why not?"

"Because everything has changed. I—we—crossed a line we never should have. I have a job to do. And it doesn't include getting involved with you. I need to maintain professional distance. Stay objective and detached."

He laughed. "I think we're way past the detached stage."

She huffed and swung her feet to the floor. "I can't do this, Greg. I can't. My teammates are the one family I've ever had. I can't lose them."

She got out of bed.

"What the hell do your teammates have to do with this?" He surged up out of the bed after her. Grabbed her by the shoulders and spun her to face him. "Tell me. I want to know!"

"They hold back the loneliness for me. They're what keeps me from becoming…you."

He stared, stricken. Ahh. Now that he understood. If her team found out she'd slept with the target, they'd ostracize her. And she'd end up alone in the wilderness, too.

"I'm sorry, Greg. Really, I am. It's all my fault. You're such a lovely man. And I took advantage of you—"

He cut her off. "Don't go all regretful and martyred on me. I was there, too, remember? I saw your passion. Heard it. Hell, *felt* it."

She stared up at him, begging silently that he stop, but he forged on. "We have something special between us. Something impossible to ignore. If you want to play this whole I shouldn't-have-slept-with-you-because-I'm-on-a-job-and-it's-unprofessional game, save it for someone else. But be honest with me. Be honest with yourself. Acknowledge your feelings for me and stop trying to fight this so damned hard."

She snatched up her clothes off the floor and headed for the bathroom.

He snagged the corner of the sheet, however, and she came up short against the end of the fabric.

"Like you're being honest with me?" she demanded.

Abandoning her cloth armor, she let go of the sheet and stomped off to the bathroom in all her naked glory.

What a woman! He could spend a lifetime sparring with her and never grow tired of her.

A lifetime—the thought brought him up short. He didn't dare think beyond tomorrow. And yet, Misty Cordell tempted him to do just that. To dare to think of next week. Next year. The rest of a long and happy life.

Shaken, he sat down hard on the edge of the bed. *How was he supposed to have a future with her when he was already a dead man walking?*

* * *

Misty fumbled awkwardly into her clothes, desperate to be covered up. To hide from the hard truths Greg was forcing her to face. She did have feelings for him. Powerful ones.

She *knew* he wasn't telling her everything. Not by a long shot. She didn't believe his glib explanation of how he'd referred to a sidewinder entirely by accident. And yet, she wanted to believe him. She'd just made wild, passionate, tender, heart-wrenching love with him, and she already wanted him again with an ache that was nearly unbearable. She wanted to march back out there, throw him down upon the bed, and have her way with him again and again until neither one of them had the strength left to talk, let alone walk.

She sat down heavily on the toilet lid. She was in deep trouble. Almost all the other Medusas had managed to juggle the requirements of a mission and their hearts at one time or another, and so far, they'd managed to come out unscathed. How had they pulled it off? Apparently, she was the one about to break that winning streak. But then, none of them had fallen in love with a spy from the other team.

She became aware of an uncomfortable bulge in her pants pocket. Her cell phone. It was late, but Vanessa wouldn't care. They were practically sisters. Misty turned on her phone, waited while it acquired a signal and dialed.

"Go," Vanessa said tersely.

"Hey. It's me."

"Misty! How are you? Where are you? Where are you headed?"

It was good to hear a friendly voice. Abjectly so. "I think I've screwed this one up, Vanessa."

Her boss answered smoothly, "Things are never as bad as they seem. We're working on sorting out the situation already. We'll figure everything out. You'll come out just fine."

"I don't think so. I've made a really big mistake this time."

"Did that guy shoot at you first?" Vanessa sounded really alarmed.

Misty frowned, confused. "What guy?"

"The one in Anchorage. The one you killed."

The abrupt shift of conversation startled Misty. "Oh. That guy. Yeah. He shot first. Used a silencer and put two shots into the wall behind the cash register. Just missed Greg."

"And then you shot back?"

"Right. Two shots. One to the forehead and a second one to the throat."

"Any reason you didn't stick around to talk to the police?"

"Besides the fact that I didn't know if Agent Smith's partner was with him to finish off the job?"

"Agent Smith?" Vanessa echoed.

"Two CIA agents who briefed me at Camp—" she barely stopped herself from slipping and naming the training facility over an unsecured line. "—you know where I mean. At any rate, they didn't introduce themselves, so I dubbed them Smith and Jones."

"You knew the guy you shot was a CIA agent?"

"Well, yes. But he shot at me first. It was a clear self-defense situation. What's the big deal?" Misty frowned at herself in the mirror above the tiny sink.

"You're being accused of murder. The police report says you fired first. They're saying you attacked the agent when you noticed him doing simple surveillance on you."

"That's a lie!" Misty exclaimed, indignant.

"There's an APB out on you in Alaska. It undoubtedly extends to the continental United States by now. General W. pulled some strings and has convinced the Canadians to hold off for a day or two in following suit. You need to head for Canada, honey. We'll meet you somewhere. Help you figure this all out."

Misty was silent, her mind racing a hundred miles an hour. They couldn't help her extricate her heart from this mission.

"Did you hear me, Sidewinder? Go to Canada."

Misty hung up, distracted, and turned off the phone. Good grief. Murder? *And she'd thought her biggest problem was sleeping with her subject.*

Back in Canada, Vanessa looked over at Isabelle grimly. "Did they get her signal?"

"Yes. She's on a boat about two hours out of Vancouver. The vessel is headed south along the coast of British Columbia. Tentative destination, Vancouver."

"Did they get an ID on the vessel?"

"They're zooming in the satellite imagery, now."

Vanessa waited tensely while her teammate stayed on the line with the NSA.

And then Isabelle announced, "It's a sport-fishing boat called the *Holy Mackerel*."

"And they'll continue to track it for us?"

"Yes."

Vanessa sighed. "Then I guess we'd better get our happy selves up to Vancouver right away."

The team burst into a flurry of controlled chaos, packing up their computers and maps with brutal efficiency. Worry nagged at the back of Vanessa's mind. When

Misty confessed to having made a big mistake, she didn't sound like she'd been referring to killing the CIA agent in Anchorage. *What else had her operator—her friend— gone and done?*

Chapter 10

Misty looked around in the predawn darkness. Her breath hung frosty in the air, and a white blanket of dew covered the grass. Her body was tired, and the cold cut through her clothing relentlessly. But her mind was on high alert. Mission alert.

The *Holy Mackerel* pulled away from the rickety dock, and Misty hoisted her backpack higher on her shoulders. She'd directed the captain to let them off some thirty miles north of Vancouver along a heavily built-up stretch of coastline. Houses crowded close, shouldering each other aside, vying for unobstructed views of the ocean. Most of them had a dock of some kind reaching out into the cold Pacific water. It was at one of these she and Greg had disembarked. Where there were houses, there were people, and where there were people, there were cars.

Greg *still* wouldn't tell her where the post office was that he needed to pick up his password at, just that it was in Vancouver somewhere. He could profess to have feelings for her all he liked, but until he backed that up with a show of real trust, she wasn't buying the line. Except her heart just wouldn't get on board with that program. As much as her head said to walk away from him, her heart ached for him…and he stood two feet away from her.

"I'll take point," she murmured.

"I bet you will."

She stopped. Turned around slowly. Took a step forward that brought her nose to nose with him. "Let's be clear, here. You've now stepped into my world. I'm in charge, and you'll do what I tell you to do when I tell you to do it. Otherwise, I'm out of here, and you can sink or swim on your own. Got it?"

"Yeah, sure," he replied. Irritably.

"You don't have to like taking orders from a woman. You don't even have to like me. But you *will* die if I bail out on you."

"What makes you so sure of that?" he snapped. "I'm not an untrained ignoramus."

"True. But I'm a trained killer. And I'll come after you myself."

He glared back at her. "That's how it's going to be? You're mad at yourself for giving in to the attraction between us, so you're going to turn into a bitch and threaten to kill me rather than face the truth of your own feelings?"

"My feelings have no place in this conversation. We're establishing a field chain of command so when the bullets start flying we know who's in charge."

"Why the hell don't your feelings have a place between

us? Are you going to pretend we didn't make passionate love to each other?"

"Jeez. You sound like a woman."

"That makes one of us, then."

She subsided, stung. After a moment, she replied grimly, "Being a Special Forces soldier is more than my job. It's who I am. It's who I choose to be. If you can't live with that, so be it. But tell ya what. You let me know when you choose who you are. I can't handle a fence-sitter."

"What the hell are you talking about?"

She couldn't believe they were standing out here on a dock in the wide open having this argument. Impatiently, she retorted, "We've got no time for this. We need to get under cover."

"I'm not leaving until you answer me. What did you mean by that?"

She huffed. "Where do your loyalties lie? Once and for all, tell me what side you're on. Right here. Right now. Do you work for the Americans or the Russians?"

He huffed back at her. "I already told you. It's not that simple."

"Sure it is. When the chips are down and you have to choose one or the other, which is it going to be? Are you on our side or their side?"

He stared at her in frustration.

"Like I said. Fence-sitter." She turned and started toward the shore. At this moment, she didn't really care if he came with her or not. His choice. Each step she took without hearing him follow her was a dagger in her heart, but she forced herself onward. She would not look back. Would not cry. She was a soldier, dammit.

Resolutely, she climbed the long steps up the cliff to

someone's backyard. It was a pretty little cottage with gingerbread trim and a neat herb garden under the kitchen window. She felt like an alien from another planet as she skirted the yard in the shadows. She would never be part of this world, so normal, so pleasant, so unassuming.

The cottage had a detached garage, which would make her job that much easier. After a quick check to verify the structure had no alarm system, she opened the garage's back door, which wasn't even locked. She couldn't imagine having that much trust in her fellow man. She slipped inside and headed for the car parked amidst the clutter of bicycles, lawnmowers, and Christmas decorations spilling out of cardboard boxes.

She reached for the door handle, and started violently as Greg brushed her hand aside. "Let me do it," he murmured.

Had he been following her all that time? She hadn't heard him, not once. She had to give him credit. He moved as quietly as a ghost. She steadfastly ignored the surge of relief fluttering in her stomach that he'd followed her at all.

Greg, seated in the driver's seat snorted, and she glanced down at him. He was holding up a key. Man, this was too easy.

"I'll go open the garage door," she murmured.

He nodded.

Apparently, they'd declared a truce. For now.

Vanessa's cell phone rang and she snatched at it. *Please be Misty.*

It wasn't. But it was the NSA. "This is Hawkeye Ops. I'm supposed to talk to a Viper."

"Speaking."

"Uhh, right."

Vanessa grinned. Folks in the business always were startled to find out they were dealing with a female special operator. "What have you got for me?"

"An update on your operative. We've been tracking her on the *Holy Mackerel*. It docked about ten minutes ago and put off two individuals, one female and one male."

"Is the female blond and gorgeous?"

"That's the one."

Vanessa glanced up and noticed the rest of the Medusas were staring at her, listening intently to her end of the conversation. Yup, they all were worried about their teammate. "Where is she now?"

"The subjects have acquired a vehicle and are on the move. They're driving south on Highway 99, leaving Britannia Beach and headed toward Vancouver."

"Vehicle description and license plate number?" Vanessa asked tersely. She whirled her finger by her ear to indicate that the team should get ready to roll. While the satellite surveillance center gave her a detailed description of a silver Honda Civic and its license plate number, the Medusas headed for the vehicles.

"Can you send us the telemetry on a mobile computer?" Vanessa asked, walking quickly.

"Yes. Once you're mobile and online, call us and we'll plug you in."

"Roger," Vanessa replied, already climbing into the driver's seat of a navy SUV. Jack would drive the other vehicle, an off-road sport truck. Isabelle rode shotgun beside her with a laptop computer on her knees. Vanessa pressed her throat microphone's transmit switch. "Radio check."

The entire team reported in.

Vanessa announced, "Sidewinder's north of Vancouver, heading our way by car. Let's move up that direction and see if we can pick her up."

Jack asked, "Are you looking to run a tail on her or apprehend her?"

"Let's play it by ear and see what her situation is first. Right now, I just want to find her."

"Roger that. Let's go get our girl."

Greg drove the car, relieved for the tense silence between them. It was better than the two of them sniping at each other out of their respective places of pain. He understood Misty's dilemma better than she knew.

He'd spent five years living in someone else's skin. But then, he'd done it voluntarily. Her own mother had thrust it upon her permanently. Nonetheless, she wasn't stuck with a bad skin to live in.

At the end of the day, she wasn't so very different from her physical appearance. Beneath her skin she was a feminine, sensuous, beautiful woman. He'd experienced her unbridled passion. And been humbled by it. For her to say she was purely a soldier was flatly untrue. It might very well be what she believed, but she was *so* much more than that.

Whether she'd let him show her that fact remained to be seen, though. Right now, he wouldn't bet good money on it. The thought of her cutting off that entire generous, loving portion of herself caused him actual pain. It was an emotional pain that reached deep down into his gut and wrenched at it.

He didn't usually run around aching for other people. In fact, he pretty much never paid attention to those sorts of things. But Misty had gotten under his skin. Which was remarkable. He didn't let people in. He didn't let *women* in. He'd been flirted with by much more accomplished temptresses than Misty Cordell, and he'd been bedded by much more willing women than her, too. But there was something about Misty…

"Turn left at the next intersection," she instructed. "We'll run into Highway 1 in about a mile. If you head south on it, you'll end up smack dab in the middle of Vancouver. From there, you're on your own to navigate since you won't tell me exactly where we're going."

"It's for your own safety, you know. It has nothing to do with me not trusting you. But if you're picked up by the authorities, the less you know, the better."

"Right."

She'd packed a world of skepticism into that single syllable. He needed to kidnap her, haul her off to some deserted island for a couple weeks, and make love to her until he'd driven away every last doubt in her mind about him. But it wasn't to be. The mission didn't allow indulgence. Always the mission, dammit.

He sighed as he made the turn. Misty wanted him to give her an answer he didn't have. His mother was American, his father Russian. He'd lived in both countries, been raised in both cultures. He considered himself to be both American and Russian.

He'd managed never to work directly against either government. They'd both employed him, but he'd always been able to position himself in assignments that hadn't forced him to betray either country. It had been a tricky juggling act, but he'd known both of his masters well enough to pull it off.

At least until the day Vasily Nemorov had died, handcuffed to his wrist. That was when he'd chosen. Or so he'd thought. He'd been fully prepared to cast his lot with the Americans until that CIA bastard shot at him in Anchorage. But now, they could all go stuff it. He'd work for himself. He'd keep the files and use them for his own ends or sell them to the highest bidder, political allegiances notwithstanding.

Of course, loyal, dutiful Misty wouldn't understand that. She'd want him to stand up and salute for the red, white and blue, come hell or high water. The Russian side of him rebelled at the thought, yet when he considered going over to the Russians for good, the American side of his soul was appalled. Besides, after stealing that MiG and fleeing Russia with some of its most classified information, he'd pretty much burned that bridge.

Which left him out in the cold.

Alone.

And that was why he could never have Misty Cordell. As much as he might want her for himself, it was not to be. He couldn't…wouldn't…ask her to leave everything she valued and walk with him into the deadly no-man's-land that awaited him.

He drove for nearly an hour, following the instructions he'd memorized before he left Russia. The sky was growing pink in the east as he pulled to a stop in a parking lot. A strip shopping center stretched away from them in both directions.

"Uhh, Greg. This isn't a post office."

"No, but that is, over there." He pointed across a wide boulevard at another, larger strip mall. From this angle they could see an open field behind it…and what were those things sticking up out of the field? He looked more closely. How appropriate. A cemetery stretched away behind the mall. Maybe a quarter mile beyond it was a subdivision full of two-story, vinyl-sided, tract homes.

He looked back at the mall. This was definitely the right address. He glanced down the crowded storefronts. There. A small place announcing itself as a quick mailing center. He explained casually, "The federal mail service in Canada requires you to sign up for a post office box in person. This place rents private mailboxes over the Internet. I got one from Moscow."

"Ahh, the wonders of modern technology. And what, exactly, did you mail to yourself?"

He glanced over at her, frowning.

"Look. I know where it is, now. I might as well know *what* it is."

He stared at her long and hard. *The moment of truth.*

The longer the moment stretched out, the more certain Misty was that he wasn't going to answer. But then Greg finally said, "It's a password, like I told you. To a file containing some data I stole from the Russian Intelligence Service."

Elation soared through her. Finally! A straight answer from the man of mystery. But more importantly, a gesture of trust. There was no room in the compact car for a happy dance, or she might bust out in one.

"Let me guess," she teased. "It contains everything a girl needs to know to build a nuclear bomb."

He smiled over at her. "Good guess."

"And why didn't you just memorize the password before you left Russian?"

"Torture."

Unfortunately, she didn't need him to explain that one. If someone unsavory had caught him and tortured him for the password to his computer, he didn't want to be able to reveal it, no matter what drugs or methods his captors tried.

"The United States isn't in the business of torturing people, you know."

"They're not my only enemy."

Her eyebrows shot up. "Last I heard, the Russian government uses some strong-arm tactics, but they're not known for torturing prisoners outright, either."

"True."

Which meant a third party was out there, gunning for him. One that wasn't a signatory to the Geneva Conventions. Which meant a private player. "Who else is after you?"

He shrugged. "Let's just say I didn't part on the best of terms with the Russian Mafia. And, if several dozen other parties were to find out the information I've collected on them, they'd be highly motivated to retrieve the information and then kill me. Slowly."

Wow. Even she and the Medusas couldn't claim that. Although she supposed if they stayed in the business a few more years they'd rack up their own who's who of bad guys out to kill them.

She asked, "Are you simply picking the password up from this private post office box, or do you have to sign for the letter?"

"Good Lord willing, it's waiting for me in my box."

"Do you have the key?"

"Around my neck."

An abrupt and vivid image of a thin chain with a small key hanging from it flashed into her head. As did the details of when and how she'd seen that key. A hot blush rushed to her cheeks.

He leaned over, cupped the back of her neck and dropped a light kiss on her temple. "I remember it, too. I will never forget our night together."

He said that like there wasn't going to be a repeat performance. Why did grief spear through her at that thought? Wasn't that what she wanted? For him to back off and keep their relationship strictly professional?

Right. And that's why her toes were curled into tight little knots of pleasure because he'd just kissed her. Yup, and she'd worked real hard to avoid that kiss, too. She was the one who'd called their making love a mistake. But was it? Had she found the right man, just in the wrong place at the wrong time?

He interrupted her turbulent thoughts by saying, "Let's go get the letter and end this thing so we can go our separate ways and get on with our lives."

She put a restraining hand on his arm as he reached for the door handle. "Not so fast."

He looked over at her in surprise. "You don't want to go our separate ways? You're the one who said we weren't meant to be."

She opened her mouth to tell him that wasn't what she was talking about. Honest. But instead, something entirely different tumbled out. "Maybe I was wrong."

He collapsed back in his seat, a thunderstruck look on his face. "Really?"

What the hell had she been thinking to say that? She'd had all the loose ends in their relationship neatly sewn up, and she'd just gone and unraveled everything again!

She replied lightly, "I know it's a shocking concept, but I do—on rare occasions—make a tiny mistake."

"Darling, in my world, throwing away the best thing ever to happen to you does not count as a tiny mistake."

Best thing ever to happen to him? *Her?* Whoa.

They stared at each other, for how long she didn't know. A long time.

"Now what?" he asked quietly.

Was he referring to them? Or to the post office box? Did she dare take the next step with him? All she had to do was tell him she felt the same way. That he'd rocked her world right down to its foundations. Forced her to seriously consider letting someone besides the Medusas into her fortress of solitude. That she wanted to spend more time with him. To get to know him better. To make love with him again.

She sighed. Said regretfully, "This mailing center place smells like a trap." *God, I'm a coward!* Disgust at herself roiled through her gut.

He replied easily enough, "And what does a trap smell like?"

Please God, don't let Greg give up on me. Please let him try again. Next time. I swear. Next time, I won't chicken out.

She frowned. "Call it healthy caution or just a gut feel, but if you waltz into that building and stroll up to your mailbox, you're going to get caught or worse."

"Who's behind this trap you smell?"

She shrugged. "No idea. You tell me. Who knows about the existence of this mailbox and has a vested interest in killing you?"

"Nobody," he blurted, startled.

"Somebody knows. Count on it. Who might that person be?"

He frowned himself. "The guy who mailed the password knows, but I'd trust him with my life."

"You have trusted him with your life. How vulnerable would this guy be to a little sodium-pentathol-assisted interrogation? Or maybe some water-boarding or a car battery attached to his privates?"

Greg winced. He saw her point. Anatoly Mityonuk was not a macho type. He was an underpaid government computer geek with a grudge against his employer. But that did not a hero make. "Okay. So we assume there's a Russian trap waiting for us in that building. How do we get in and get my letter?"

"First order of business is to set up surveillance on the place. And fortunately, we're already ideally located to do that. I'd suggest we hunker down here for a while and get a feel for the place."

"It won't open for several hours."

"All the better," she replied. "We can watch the employees come in."

They sat there for several hours as the sun came up and a steady flow of customers went in and out of the mail center. For the life of him, he didn't see anything the slightest bit out of the ordinary. But Misty remained jumpy, insisting that something was wrong that she couldn't put her finger on.

And then she turned on her cell phone and dialed directory assistance. He listened, perplexed, as she got the mail store's phone number and dialed it.

"Hi, this is Cathy. Is Crispy there?…That's his nickname. I dunno his real name. He gave me this phone number. He's the new guy…."

There was a lengthy pause while she listened, and her expression grew more grim by the second. Not good.

She replied, "No, I want the tall one…Samuel, huh? He doesn't seem like a Samuel….comes on at noon? I'll call back then. Thanks."

She hung up and looked over at him grimly. "Two of their employees up and quit all of a sudden a couple days ago. But lucky for the owner, a couple of other guys just happened to walk in asking after jobs. They're working out great so far."

He snorted. "I bet. I hear intelligence agents make pretty good mail-room guys."

"Let's get out of here. I've seen enough."

"Enough for what?"

"Enough to plan the next step. We can't make a direct approach, so let's back off, regroup and plan this thing before we barge in and get in trouble. Trust me."

Trust her.

Did he trust her?

She'd talked him down out of the sky when he'd been shot and disoriented. She'd yanked him out of bed in the hospital when the fake nurse had tried to shoot him. She'd killed a CIA agent for him. She'd made love with him, for God's sake. Had looked him in the eyes and shown her naked soul to him. Why wouldn't he trust her?

She'd steadfastly demonstrated to him from the first moment in the sky over Alaska when she'd jumped onto the radios to translate for him that he was not alone.

He released a long, slow breath. A great weight fell away from his chest as he let go—finally—of five long years' worth of paranoia. Of isolation. Of fear.

"Where do you suggest we go?" he asked quietly.

"Let's head for a hotel. One with Internet service. We have some research to do."

Vanessa put down her binoculars just as Jack radioed her from his position on the far side of the parking lot.

"Scat here. They've started the car. They're leaving. Either they missed a rendezvous or they're spooked. What's the call, boss? Do we close in or keep the surveillance net loose around them for now?"

Vanessa grinned. *As if anyone would ever be Jack Scatalone's boss.* He was his own man. Always would be. But then, she was her own woman, too. That was why they made a great pair.

"Let's stand off for now. I don't know what they're doing, but they're definitely up to something. They're acting like they've got company. Has anyone spotted any indications of another surveillance operation or ambush out here?"

Silence met her question, which constituted a no from everyone on her team.

She commented, "Best case—we let this scenario roll and it helps exonerate Misty."

"Worst case—it'll be the last nail in her coffin," Jack replied heavily.

Chapter 11

Misty crouched behind a commercial air conditioning unit beside Greg. They were on the roof of the strip mall, and the wind was sharp with cold. Clouds still covered the moon, but the way this cold front was blowing in, they wouldn't have deep darkness for too much longer. Man-sized metal heating and cooling units cast shadows within shadows across the expanse of roof before them. It was a great place to run an urban stealth op.

Getting up here hadn't been hard. They'd crawled through the cemetery behind the mall to the narrow alley at one end. She'd hung climbing ropes for them and she and Greg had walked up the side of the building. Literally.

"Ready to rock and roll?" she murmured into her headset. They'd found these mini walkie-talkies at a sporting goods store. They hooked over the ear, and a thin boom stretched down to the corner of the mouth. They weren't anywhere near as good as the throat mikes the Medusas used, but they were better than nothing.

"Let's do it," he replied confidently.

Greg had been shockingly cooperative all day as she planned tonight's op. Either he was up to some new head game with her or they'd turned some sort of corner in their relationship. Frankly, she wasn't sure which one she preferred right now. Her heart shouted its hope that he hadn't given up on her. She desperately wanted him to trust her and care for her. But right now, in her head—in her soldier persona—she needed him to follow orders and keep his feelings to himself. It felt as if she was being torn in two. Good thing she'd been trained to work under extreme duress, because by golly, she was there.

She eased forward on her hands and knees.

"This crawling is killing my thigh. Wouldn't it be faster if we walked?" Greg murmured.

"Absolutely. It also would make our silhouettes easy to spot. If the Russians have gone to all the trouble to plant two employees in this store, you can count on 'round the clock surveillance on the place. If your leg is giving you too much trouble, I'll continue alone. Just let me know."

"I'm not letting you do this alone. No way!"

She nodded, and paused for a moment to give his injured thigh a rest. "We have to assume this area's being watched. That's why we've got to stay low. And hey, at least I got you knee pads."

He chuckled ruefully. "I can't wait to see what you have in mind for all this rope we've still got left."

"Easy. We're going in through the ceiling of the mail store."

He groaned. "I hoped you weren't serious about that part when you went through the plan earlier."

"Those vans parked along the back of the mall worry me. Without infrared scanning gear, I can't check through their skins for hostiles. If the vans weren't there, we could try going in through the mail store's back door. Although, the problem with that idea is I don't have my usual complement of gadgets to get around the place's security system."

He sighed but didn't complain.

Her knees ached before long, even with the knee pads. She paused near the edge of the roof, behind a giant piece of galvanized metal ducting, to have another look down at the service road behind the mall. No movement drew her scanning gaze. If someone was out there, they were hunkered down out of sight, watching. Hopefully, the Russians were shy on manpower and only had one guy in front of the mall and one out back. If there were only one guy back here, she'd bet her next paycheck he was in one of those vans.

Greg crawled up beside her and flopped down, shoulder to shoulder. As quickly as the night's cold was soaking through her clothes, warmth from his big, sturdy body infused her. She had to give him credit. He wasn't complaining about his thigh, and it had to hurt. She glanced over at him and he smiled back at her.

"Having fun?" he murmured.

"Actually, yes. I love this stuff."

He replied lightly, "In all my years of searching for true love, I have *never* met a woman like you."

"You haven't met my teammates, then."

"There are more women special operators like you?"

She nodded.

"A mind-boggling concept."

She grinned at him. "Most of them have found true love already, though."

His voice dropped to a deep, low rumble in her ear. "I don't need to meet any others to know which one I'm interested in."

Relief swept over her, like a flash flood, making her hot and cold all over. *He's still interested in me.* She hadn't driven him away after all. "You have no idea how glad I am to hear you say that."

He leaned down and dropped a quick kiss on her surprised mouth.

"Do that again," she breathed.

"Don't we have a job to do?"

She blinked a couple of times while she tried to clear her head. "Later," she mumbled.

"Count on it," he murmured back.

"General Karkarov, I have an overseas call for you. Top priority."

He looked up irritably from his supper at Gennady. That boy lived to make his life hell. "Who is it?"

"The Spetznatz team in Vancouver. They may have spotted your man and they need final permission to kill him."

It was a hell of a stupid way to run an army, to have units in the fields calling generals at home in Moscow for permission to do their damned jobs. "Patch them through," he growled.

Gennady hustled forward with a phone in hand. "Here they are, sir."

"Go ahead. This is Karkarov."

A scratchy voice at the other end reported crisply,

"We have possible target acquisition. Require final approval for the kill."

"Approval granted. Take that bastard out. And call me when you've confirmed he's dead."

"Understood."

"Good shooting," the general replied grimly.

Humming from head to toe, Misty moved out, heading for the middle of the mall roof and the location of the mail store. Greg stretched out beside her again, and set her body vibrating anew by his mere presence beside her. If she thought she had any chance of suppressing her visceral reaction to him, she'd do her darnedest to conquer it. But as it was, she didn't waste the time or energy even trying.

"We'll set escape ropes here," she breathed. Part of her training was always, always to have a plan B in place. In this case, a set of rappelling ropes off the roof.

Greg nodded tersely at her. He was a professional and understood the need for both of them to concentrate completely on the task at hand now. She anchored the grappling hooks and inertia reels attached to each of their climbing ropes and laid out the lengths of heavy nylon so they wouldn't tangle if a person took a running leap off the roof. The inertia reels would gradually break the fall of a person on the other end of the rope. She set the catch point carefully so they'd slow down about six feet above the ground.

"If we need to bug out, slap the clip at the end of the rope to your climbing harness and jump."

He grimaced. "It's that jumping part that's got me worried."

"The inertia reel will catch you. Trust me."

His smile flashed in the darkness. "Fine. I trust you."

"Harness check," she ordered. His hands skimmed over

her climbing harness, flat nylon straps cupping her behind
and wrapping around the tops of her thighs. His fingers
paused on the buckle at her waist, slipping between her
waist and the buckle. And then it was her turn to do the
same to him. His body was so hard. So male. Sculpted
muscles slid under her palms like a fine statue. Her fingers
curled around his harness buckle against his belly, and oh
my, the tension was just right. The buckle was adjusted
properly, too.

"Let's go," she mumbled, flustered.

They reached the fifth air conditioner on the right and
continued on for another twenty feet or so, which should
place them directly over the mail store. It also placed them
out on a wide-open stretch of roof. She glanced up at the
clouds, which were thinning by the second.

"Now what?" he whispered.

"Look for an access panel. There's got to be one around
her somewhere. It'll look like a hatch of some kind."

"Got it. Find a hatch."

"Stay low. We're way exposed out here."

He paused to squeeze her hand. "Thanks for worrying
about me. I'm worried about you, too."

"Stay alive, will ya?"

He smiled gently at her. "You too."

Her insides curled into happy little knots this time.
They crawled around on their bellies for several minutes,
dragging themselves across the scratchy tar and asphalt
roof. Finally, Greg murmured in her earpiece, "Found it."

She joined him, not far from the alley edge of the
roof. "While I open this, you keep watch out below for
any movement."

He nodded and slithered away to take up a position at
the edge of the roof.

She pulled out the lock picks she'd picked up that afternoon and went to work on the heavy padlock. This thing was going to be a bear to open. But that's what she got paid the big bucks for. Or something like that. Too bad Aleesha wasn't here. That woman could open any lock in creation in under a minute.

It took Misty nearly ten minutes, but finally, the padlock gave a satisfying click and popped open. Yes. She opened the metal trapdoor carefully, laying it down gently on the roof. Metal stairs led down into the mall's attic.

She tapped Greg's foot. When he glanced back over his shoulder, she gestured for him to join her. The two of them eased down into the black cavern of steel rafters, insulation and ducting. Walking along a steel I-beam like a gymnast on a balance beam, she made her way back to her left and the mail store, if her estimate was correct. It was a simple matter to locate another access panel down into the mail store itself. To make it even simpler, it had no lock. It would lift out easily when the time came.

"You know the plan," she murmured. "We'll drop the last set of ropes, rappel down at warp speed, grab the letter, and shimmy up and out of there as fast as humanly possible. Just because we don't hear anything doesn't mean there won't be a silent alarm going off somewhere else inconvenient, like a police station or a Russian surveillance vehicle right out front."

He finished tying off their climbing ropes to a steel cross beam and flashed her a thumbs-up. "Ready," he announced.

"Here goes." She lifted the access panel and set it aside. A quick peek below. No red laser beams criss-crossing the store. That didn't mean there weren't infrared motion detectors down there, though. She tossed down the ropes and helped Greg ease over the edge of the opening and onto the rope. He hand-over-handed a couple times and then dropped the rest of the way to the floor. She followed as soon as he was out of the way, dropping lightly onto the balls of her feet. Greg was already heading toward the front of the store.

"Problem," he called out low. "There's a security grille between us and the mailboxes."

Damn. She'd been hoping they'd come out on the other side of such a divider. She went to work on the key lock holding it in place. It wasn't quite as elaborate an affair as the padlock and took her about thirty seconds. Greg pushed open the steel screen and slipped through the opening. She glided to the front of the store, sticking to a shadow as she approached the plate-glass windows.

A van sat all alone out front, parked about halfway between the store and the street. Not good. Not at this time of night, and not all alone like that.

She heard a metal door open behind her. "Is it in there?"

He laughed. "Would you believe I've got junk mail?"

"Yes, I would. The letter?" She glanced over her shoulder and saw him rifling through a stack of flyers and catalogs. "We may have a problem."

He glanced up quickly. "What kind of problem?"

"Company."

The driver's door of the van opened. A tall, black-garbed figure got out.

Started walking toward the store. *Crap.*

"One hostile incoming. *We need to go.*"

She eased backward, away from the window.

"Got it!" Greg exclaimed.

The man reached inside his jacket and pulled out a dark, blunt shape. Gun.

"Run!"

Greg darted for the back of the store.

"Start climbing," she ordered. "I'll cover you." Not that she had a whole lot of firepower to cover him with. But she'd buy him the time he needed to get up that rope. She yanked the steel grille shut and threw the bolt. She jumped for her rope and saw Greg's legs just disappearing into the hole in the ceiling. She jumped up, grabbing the rope as high as she could and started pulling herself up hand-over-hand.

The front door rattled. She swore under her breath.

A burst of wind and cold air announced that the dark figure had let himself into the store. Which meant he had keys to the place. She grabbed tight with her left hand and let go of the rope with her right. Hanging by one hand, she awkwardly reached around her torso and pulled her Glock out of the shoulder holster she'd bought earlier. Twisting slowly on the rope, she took aim and fired at the deadbolt holding the security grille shut. Sparks flew and the noise was deafening in the confined space.

She slammed the gun back into her holster and commenced climbing again as the dark figure got up from where he'd dropped flat on the floor. An arm extended through the grille. She heaved, setting herself swinging as she frantically climbed the last few feet of the rope. Two bullets winged past her, the muzzle flashes blinding in the dark. That second shot had been close. She'd felt the wind of its passage. Twisting and jerking herself higher simultaneously, she reached the edge of the access hole. Strong hands grabbed her wrists and gave her a mighty yank. She tumbled onto the roofing material, landing on top of Greg.

"Roll!" she shouted.

She flung herself sideways, wrapping her arms around

Greg and bodily dragging him with her. The ceiling exploded as bullets tore through where they'd been lying an instant before.

They clambered to their feet in the dark and scrambled over and under steel support beams toward the faint square of night light coming through the roof access panel. They ran up the narrow metal steps, their feet clattering obscenely loudly. They burst onto the roof and dived for the deep shadow of the nearest air conditioner.

"Now what?" he panted.

"We've got to get off this roof. We're sitting ducks up here. They can surround us and shoot us."

"The escape ropes," he bit out grimly.

She nodded and they took off running, crouching low and zigzagging from shadow to shadow. Misty looked around frantically as she ran. She had the distinct sensation they weren't alone up here, but she didn't see anyone. Must be the adrenaline talking.

They grabbed the clips she'd laid out so carefully earlier, slammed them onto the loops at their waists and ran for the edge of the roof. As one, they jumped out into space. The reels sang like hot metal zinging against cold steel as the rope played out through their pulleys and brakes. Her climbing harness caught, tightened, and lurched as her fall broke into a semi-controlled crash. She absorbed the remaining impact with her knees, landing on her feet and collapsing into a tight tuck and roll. She let the momentum carry her all the way over and back onto her feet. She sprang up, ready to run. She unclipped the rope and looked around for Greg. He was just fumbling at his own climbing harness.

Footsteps pounded from the far end of the alley. A man was running at them, a delivery van's side door open behind him. Yup, surveillance van. Dammit, she hated being right about stuff like that.

"Let's go," she bit out.

They'd discussed their emergency egress plan earlier and Greg knew to head for the cemetery. The running man lifted a long, bulky shape away from his side. Misty swore under her breath.

"Hit the dirt!" she yelled as a semiautomatic machine gun ripped off a fusillade of lead, shattering the silence. "Roll for the fence!"

They had to get out of this narrow strip of asphalt and concrete. They were dead if they didn't reach cover—and soon. She log-rolled as fast as she could, eating gravel and dirt and scratching the hell out of every bit of exposed skin.

A shout from the other direction. Crud. In Russian. The guy from the front of the mail store must have run around back and was entering the alley from the other end. The good news: it bought them a momentary reprieve. The two Russians had conflicting fields of fire. They couldn't fire their weapons at her and Greg lest they take out each other.

And then another sound split the night, ten times more ominous than anything she'd heard so far. The distinctive slap of ropes—lots of them—hitting the wall behind her and the slithering hiss of inertia reels unwinding. She risked a glance over her shoulder and gasped. No less than seven ninja-black figures had just jumped off the roof. As Misty watched in dismay, they raced outward in a textbook-perfect fighting formation, spraying gunfire in a deadly blossom of lead that eradicated the two Russians as easily as slapping a mosquito. And then the weapons turned on her and Greg.

They were so hosed.

Without waiting for the commandos to say a thing, she froze on her stomach, reaching up slowly over her head and laying her Glock flat on the ground.

She said quietly, "It's over, Greg. Don't move."

Chapter 12

One of the largest of the dark figures gestured with the muzzle of his MP-5 for them to climb to their feet. Greg eyed the guy and complied carefully, easing closer to stand beside Misty. If these bastards started firing, maybe he could jump in front of her and fall on top of her. It wasn't much, but it was the best he could do to protect her under the circumstances.

Who the hell were these guys? Russians? CIA? He'd assumed the two men who'd initially rushed them were Russians, but maybe not. Maybe they'd been the American surveillance and this bunch was a Spetznatz unit dispatched to clean up the mess that was Vasily Nemorov/Greg Mitchell. Funny that neither identity was actually him. And yet, he was about to die for being both men.

The muzzle of the MP-5 that he couldn't seem to take his eye off of jerked to the left.

"C'mon," Misty mumbled in Russian. "If they're not going to shoot us here and now, we've got nothing to lose by going with them. You don't happen to have a cyanide tooth do you?"

"No. You?"

"Negative."

"I don't want them to torture you. Let's make our stand here," he argued.

"These guys want something. We can bargain with the computer for our lives."

He was startled that nobody barked at the two of them to be silent, but then the team closed in on them—as in bodily crowding against him and Misty—and all but lifted them forward toward the near end of the alley. A step van drove around the corner, its lights out.

It pulled just past them and stopped. Another black-garbed figure threw open the back door and he and Misty were physically lifted inside the vehicle. He slammed into the cold metal floor uncomfortably. He half rolled until he ran into Misty. The comfort of her familiar curves against him cleared his head. He and Misty did, indeed, have a powerful bargaining chip on their side. They knew where the computer with its incredible hoard of information was stashed. The trick now would be to live long enough to get to bargain with it for our lives.

The team of commandos piled in the van after them and the door slammed shut. The floor jerked as the van lurched into motion. One of the commandos pulled a heavy, rubber curtain across the front of the cargo space, blocking out the front windows entirely. The interior went pitch-black. The van bumped over a couple of potholes, then turned right and accelerated on smooth pavement. Someone turned on a red light of some kind that bathed the entire back of the van in a hellish glow.

And then the damnedest thing happened. One of the commandos reached up and pulled off his cloth head mask.

Misty swore under her breath. Colorfully.

And then all the commandos pulled off their masks. And half of them were women!

Misty started to laugh beside him. She was laughing? Had she lost her mind? He noticed the commandos were grinning, too. Had they all lost their minds?

Then Misty gasped between fits of laughter, "Man, am I glad to see all of you."

He burst out, "Would somebody please let me in on the joke?"

"Greg, meet the Medusas. Friends."

The Medusas? *The* Medusas? *Misty Cordell is a Medusa?* When a report had come across his Moscow desk from a low-level Pentagon informant asserting that the United States had formed an all-female Special Forces team, he'd all but laughed aloud. He'd filed the report in his list of interesting but uncorroborated tidbits and hadn't forwarded it to his superiors. There'd been no need to get himself laughed out of the Kremlin. Besides, if by some strange twist of fate the report were true, the U. S. would certainly want the team's existence kept secret. So, he'd buried the report.

No wonder Misty had gone nuts when he made the sidewinder reference. The Medusa report had mentioned a rumor that the operatives all used snake species as their field handles. And no wonder she'd killed with such cool efficiency. She was everything she'd said she was and more. Much more.

Misty continued with the introductions. "This is our team leader, Vanessa Blake."

An attractive woman on the end of the bench in front of him nodded.

"Her husband and our boss, Jack Scatalone."

The tall guy who'd done the gesturing with the MP-5 nodded from beside the Blake woman. Misty went around the van and introduced a total of five women and four men, including the petite Asian woman driving the van and the tall blond woman navigating beside her.

Misty concluded with, "And this is Gregorii Harkov."

Vanessa nodded brusquely. "You've caused quite a ruckus, Mr. Harkov. Our girl, Misty, is in a bit of a bind because of you."

Misty blurted, "I volunteered for this. Greg never asked me to run with him. In fact, he tried hard to get rid of me. I insisted on sticking with him."

The Blake woman's eyebrows shot straight up, and her intelligent gaze flitted back and forth between him and Misty. He got the distinct impression the nature of their relationship was no secret any more to Misty's boss. His face heated up. Thankfully it was too dim and red in here for his blush to be seen.

Misty sat up, and he did the same. The metal floor was cold and hard, but his relief at not being the prisoner of a group of motivated killers was too intense for him to care. Although, on second thought, maybe he *was* in the presence of motivated killers.

"Hey, Python!" Misty called.

The blonde in the passenger seat looked over her shoulder questioningly.

"We need to swing by our hotel to pick up some gear."

"How soon?" the blonde asked.

Misty grimaced. "ASAP."

The blonde nodded. Greg's jaw dropped as the blond directed the driver, "Turn left at the next light. We need to loop back to the north to get to the Thunderbird Motel."

"How in the hell do you know what hotel we're staying at?" he demanded.

The blonde smiled at him grimly. She turned the laptop computer on her knees so he could see the screen. A bird's-eye view of a van driving down a highway glowed back at him. "We've been watching you since yesterday. The resolution on this camera is so good we could see you wipe your nose."

His jaw dropped. "Where'd you get that?"

Misty answered from beside him. "Satellite feed. I should've figured. You picked us up when I called you, didn't you?" she accused her boss.

Vanessa Blake nodded.

He interrupted. "You've been tracking us with a satellite for over a day?" Tying up a resource like that for an entire day took unbelievable clout…or a no-kidding matter of national security. Without waiting for anyone to answer, he turned to the Blake woman. "Who are you people? Who do you work for?"

The major answered him evenly, "We are a Special Forces team. And we work for the President of the United States."

"What agency do you work for? Are you CIA?"

The woman shrugged. "After 9/11, the sharp lines between different agencies of the federal government have blurred considerably. Where it once made a big difference whether a person worked for the Department of Defense or the FBI or the CIA, we're more or less one big happy family these days."

He'd left the States before the terrorist attack, and

frankly, he had a hard time conceiving of the unification she described having taken place so quickly.

The van accelerated out onto a highway and Vanessa leaned forward intently. "We need to know exactly what happened in Anchorage. What can the two of you tell us?"

Misty murmured to him in Russian, "You first."

He spoke up in English. It felt strange on his tongue to hold an actual conversation in that language. He hadn't used it except in short snatches for years. He spoke haltingly. "We went to an electronics store to get some supplies—"

"For what?" Vanessa interrupted. "We have a list of the stuff you bought."

He glanced over at Misty and she nodded. He answered, "To charge the battery on a computer."

"Then what?" Vanessa asked.

"I was at the cash register paying for our purchases when there was a loud noise of glass breaking. I looked around and saw the front window had shattered. I heard another noise—this time of a bullet hitting wood. It's a cracking noise combined with a sort of dull thud—"

"I know the sound," Vanessa interjected dryly. "Go on."

"I hit the floor and yelled for the proprietor to do the same. Misty crawled over to me. Then I noticed a woman standing in the middle of the store, right in the apparent line of fire. She'd frozen."

Nods all around, as though these folks encountered that sort of thing often in their line of work.

"I tackled her and guided her to a storeroom in the back of the store."

Misty took up the narrative. "I crawled over to the front window and spotted the shooter. Like I told General Wittenauer, when the guy popped up and took another shot at me, I recognized him. He was one of two CIA agents who briefed me about Greg at Camp Green. Next time he popped up to shoot, I took him out. A chest shot. I didn't confirm the kill, but I understand he's dead."

"Oh, he's dead, all right," Vanessa commented. "And the CIA's jonesing to catch you and charge you with murder."

Greg frowned. "But he shot at us first. How come that's not self-defense?"

Vanessa shrugged. "Assuming you two are telling the truth, and I have no reason to believe you're not, the evidence at the scene has been tampered with."

"Why?" Greg demanded.

"You tell me."

Misty piped up. "Greg brought some sensitive information out of Russia with him. We knew the Russians would try to kill him. But why the CIA?"

Greg bit out in Russian, "I don't trust these people. Don't say so much."

She snapped back in the same tongue, "I *do* trust them. This is my family. I trust these people with my life."

"They're federal employees. I bet they've got orders to kill us both if we pose a threat to their precious government."

"So what if they do? I'd kill you if you posed a threat to my government."

He lurched as though she'd struck him. "So making love with me truly meant nothing to you?"

She sat back hard herself. "It meant everything to me! But I can't betray my country!"

He asked lightly, "So. Does sleeping with an enemy of the State constitute treason these days?"

"Why?" she asked back, matching his sarcasm. "Are you concerned you'll get in trouble with the Kremlin for sleeping with me?"

She looked nearly as frustrated as he felt. He huffed. "I don't work for the Kremlin any more."

As he expected, she jumped all over that. "Do you work for the United States, then?"

"I didn't say that."

"Dammit, who do you work for?" she burst out.

"Look. The CIA tried to kill me. Even if I was loyal to the Americans, how am I supposed to feel about them now? They tried to kill me, Misty."

She switched to English and looked up at her boss. "Viper, what does the CIA say about why its guy shot at us?"

Greg glanced up. He'd forgotten for a moment the others were there. Thankfully, none of them seemed to have understood their argument in Russian.

"Nothing, other than they're pissed off you took out someone from the home team."

"We need to know who gave the order to shoot and why," Misty said heavily.

"Talk to me," Vanessa urged. "What's going on?"

Misty shrugged. "If the order to kill Greg came from high levels within the CIA, then we've got a problem. They've made false assumptions about Greg that we're going to have to correct. If a rogue agent shot at Greg on his own, then the CIA simply needs to acknowledge it had a bad egg in its midst. It's possible the shooter acted entirely on his own. Maybe he was a double agent. Maybe he was simply for sale to a sweet enough offer."

A double agent? He hadn't thought of that. But why not? After all, there'd been one double agent in the hospital in Alaska. Why not a second sleeper agent inside the CIA?

"What side of the motel are you two on?" the petite Asian woman called from the front seat.

"The east side," Misty called back.

The van pulled to a stop. The engine cut off.

"We'll go in alone," Misty murmured. "You guys look like ninjas in those get-ups. If someone sees you, they'll call the police."

The others grinned. He and Misty climbed out of the van and walked quickly to their door. Misty pulled out the room key and they slipped inside. She turned on the light and headed straight for her backpack. She started stuffing tools and gear into it.

He stood still by the door. After a moment, she glanced over at him. "What?"

"We can make a break for it. Just the two of us. We can work our way down the connecting doors like we did before."

She snorted. "So the guys operating the satellite can call them and tell them which end of the building to pick us up at?"

He huffed. "We can disguise ourselves. You and I are smart enough to give these guys the slip."

She frowned. "Why would I want to do that? With their help, we can get this whole mess straightened out. They've got the resources and smarts to help us get your files out of the computer and to set the record straight on the Anchorage shooting."

"They work for the same government that's trying to kill me and charge you with murder!"

"And until I know why, I'm not willing to declare the entire U.S. government our enemy."

Our enemy? She'd cast her lot with him, then? His anger evaporated as fast as it had formed. She moved over to him and looped her arms around his waist. "Trust me, Greg. Trust them. The Medusas won't let you down."

He wrapped her up and held her tight.

She squeezed him tighter, burrowing against his chest the same way she'd burrowed right into his heart.

He sighed. "We better get going."

"I'd hate to have Viper walk in on us like this."

He grinned down at her wryly. "I seriously doubt our feelings for each other are any secret to her."

Misty was alarmed. "Why do you say that?"

"Have you seen the way she looks at her husband? She knows exactly what the pull between us feels like."

"God, it's like having five meddling sisters and four big brothers looking over my shoulder."

He laughed. "Family isn't such a bad thing. If I had one, I'd look forward to sharing the news that I'd found you."

Pink suffused her cheeks as she whirled away. "You get the computer and I'll get the rest of the gear."

He grinned knowingly. There she went again. Retreating into the mission to avoid acknowledging her true feelings. The two of them weren't so very different in that regard.

They wiped the room down for fingerprints and left the room key on the bathroom counter, then they glided through the shadows to the step van and climbed inside.

"Now where?" Vanessa asked.

Greg shrugged. "Somewhere with a good supply of electricity, a tool bench and some privacy."

Vanessa said briskly, "General Wittenauer's in Seattle. Let's join up with him. I suspect we're going to need his help sorting out the mess over at CIA."

The driver nodded and headed out. They'd passed through Vancouver and were headed south on a smooth highway toward the U.S. border when the woman driving announced quietly, "We've got company."

Chapter 13

Misty lurched at Katrina Kim's announcement. "Are they closing on us?"

"Nope. Hanging back. Tailing us for now."

Isabelle turned off the red light and Misty peeled up a corner of the rubber cloth taped over the van's back window to peer outside. "Can we lose them at the border?"

Vanessa shrugged. "Maybe. Depends on how they're tracking us. Question is, do we want to lose them? With the firepower we've got, maybe we should go ahead and suck them in."

Misty considered the suggestion. It had merit. She was no big fan of running interminably if the pursuer could be trapped, bagged and tagged instead.

"Are you nuts?" Greg burst out. "These guys are killers!"

Misty glanced at him. "What are we? Chopped liver?"

He shrugged. "You tell me. All I saw in the Russian report on the Medusas was that they were a prototype team being trained as an experiment to see if women could cut it in Special Forces or not. Can you cut it?"

Vanessa and Jack both surged across the van, but Jack got to Greg first and grabbed a fistful of shirt. He growled, "Where in the hell did you hear about the Medusas?"

Misty leaped forward. "Stand down, Scat. He's on our side." *She hoped.*

Jack let go of Greg and subsided back onto a bench, but continued to glare. Thankfully, Misty noted that Greg looked unruffled as he replied calmly, "If you can help me retrieve the data out of my computer, I'll *give* you the file on your snake ladies. It came to Moscow from someone who works with the Pentagon's super-computer array."

Vanessa breathed, "Jerry the Wonder Hacker. I'd lay odds on it. He's just slimy enough to sell us out."

Jack replied in surprise, "Aren't you friends with him?"

Vanessa snorted. "He'd sell out his own mother for the right price."

Greg nodded, "I do recall a notation that the source was paid. It was a straight information-for-money deal."

Misty interjected, "Do you remember anything else?"

Greg shrugged. "I didn't pass the file up the chain of command. I didn't think anyone in the Kremlin would believe it. And, if it *was* true, the Russians didn't need to know about it."

Misty breathed a sigh of relief that everyone else matched, but additionally, she gave him a long, hard look. If he'd protected the Medusas by burying that report, maybe he *had* been trying to work for the Americans like he said. And just maybe he'd been telling her the truth earlier. She couldn't blame him for being cautious after that CIA agent shot at him, though.

Vanessa pulled out her cell phone and placed a phone call. "Sir, it's me."

She must be talking to General Wittenauer.

"Yes, we've got the whole package. We're going to need a computer lab when we arrive at your end…. Yes, sir. They say the CIA agent shot first…. Yes, they'll swear to it. There was another witness besides the store clerk, too. A female customer who wasn't mentioned in the police report. If we can track her down, maybe she can corroborate their story…. That's correct."

The anvil that had been sitting on Misty's chest for the past couple days was starting to lift away. Dang, it was a relief to have her teammates on her side and applying their considerable assistance to her problem. Now, if only they could get Greg to declare which side of the fence his loyalties fell on once and for all.

Vanessa was talking again. "…need expedited clearance across the border. We've picked up a tail and need to lose him…. Sorry, I never promised we'd be easy to work with."

Vanessa disconnected the call. "He told us to head for the commercial vehicle lane when we hit the border crossing. He'll take care of everything else."

Misty shuddered. She hated to think of how many favors the general was burning on her. Ah well. All for one and one for all didn't only apply when everything was going peachy.

"Get some sleep everyone," Vanessa ordered. "Cobra, let me know when you want a break."

Katrina nodded from the driver's seat.

Misty leaned back against the van's wall and closed her

eyes. Sleep claimed her almost immediately. She regained enough consciousness at some point to realize she was snuggled against Greg's shoulder with his arm around her. How she'd gotten there, she had no idea. She closed her eyes and drifted back to sleep.

General Wittenauer must have seriously greased the wheels at the border because Misty was able to sleep through the entire crossing. One minute she was dozing on Greg's chest, and the next, Katrina was murmuring quietly, "Ten minutes to the safe house, Viper."

Misty felt a hundred percent better after the power nap. She'd been stunned during her initial Medusa training to realize how little sleep a human being could function on if necessary.

Vanessa checked all around to make sure everyone was awake, then said tersely in her mission voice, "We'll back the van right up to the house and fan out in a personnel security formation. Once the perimeter is secure, Jack and Dex will offload Misty and Greg directly into the garage. General Wittenauer says the van will be too tall to pull inside."

Nods all around.

"Python, Mamba, I need you two to go ahead and clear the house."

Karen and Aleesha nodded their understanding.

Vanessa added, "General Wittenauer may be inside, so announce yourselves and don't shoot the boss, eh? Even if he says it's clean, I want you to check the place out from top to bottom. And close all the curtains while you're at it."

Karen, who was still recovering from her poison-induced heart attack, and Aleesha, who'd been shot on their last mission, grimaced. Misty sympathized. In their line of work, the invalids got stuck with all the boring jobs. "Where is this house, anyway?"

"Down the coast a little ways from Seattle. General Wittenauer got some computer big shot to lend him his weekend place for a few days."

Dang, that man had connections. After thirty years in the Special Forces business, she supposed a whole lot of people owed him favors, though.

When they turned into the driveway, Misty gaped along with everyone else through the front of the van. *Some weekend place.* She'd bet it had at least twelve bedrooms. It was a huge, ultra-modern mansion of glass and concrete, right out of the pages of a design magazine. And this was just the owner's beach house? Cripes. When Vanessa said a big shot owned this place, she wasn't kidding!

The maneuver went off as smooth as silk. The only delay was that it took Karen and Aleesha, augmented by Kat and Isabelle, nearly a half hour to clear the entire structure. But eventually, Misty and Greg stood in a modern kitchen gleaming with stainless steel and polished granite. General Wittenauer was on the phone, and he'd waved them into the room while arguing with someone at the other end.

He cut off the call in disgust. "Damned Harvard weenies infesting Langley," he growled.

Misty laughed, "And here we were, trying so hard to convince Greg that everyone in the U.S. government shares their toys and plays nicely with the other children these days."

Wittenauer rolled his eyes and stood up. He looked like he wanted to hug her, but stopped just short of doing it. "Glad to see you, girl. You've had us worried."

Her heart swelled. This man was as close to a father as

she'd had since she was a child. "Sir, this is Greg Harkov. Greg, General Wittenauer."

"Harkov? I thought your name was Mitchell."

"That was my CIA legend. I was born in Russia, son of Milo Ilyich Harkov."

Wittenauer swore under his breath. "Those CIA bastards are holding out on me."

Vanessa laughed. "So call the boss. He can get straight answers for you."

Misty bet he could. Vanessa was referring to the boss. The President of the United States. In point of technical fact, the Medusas worked directly for him.

Wittenauer rolled his eyes. "Don't tempt me. So. Where are we?"

Vanessa filled him in quickly on the details she hadn't told him on the phone.

Wittenauer looked over at Greg. "Mind if I ask why you need a computer lab?"

The sudden tension that rolled off of Greg slammed into Misty. "There's some data on a computer I brought out with me. I need to retrieve it."

"Downstairs. The girls can show you where it is."

Aleesha laughed. "It's practically got a mainframe down there. But me t'inks it be runnin' de whole house, mon."

Greg replied, "I just need power outlets and voltage regulators. If my contact sent me the right password, the data should be a piece of cake to recover."

Misty put a hand on his arm. "Let us help you. Between the lot of us, we know a fair bit about computers. More to the point, we know a fair bit about breaking into them."

Greg shrugged. "The more the merrier."

The group trooped downstairs to a state-of-the-art

computer lab. A workbench dominated one side of the clean room, and shelves storing a mind-numbing array of parts and accessories lined the opposite wall. It was a good-sized space, but ten people made for a tight fit. Quickly, Greg relayed what he knew of the magnetic screws holding the computer case shut, the acid foam that would release onto the hard drive if they screwed up, the oddball operating frequency, and the password he hoped was in his letter from Anatoly.

While the others discussed options for electrifying the screws to fake them into believing they were still attached, Misty surveyed the parts and tools lining the walls. "What about using this?" She picked up what looked like a miniature welding torch.

"To do what?" Greg asked.

"Cut through the case. Leave the screws right where they are and cut around them."

Greg nodded, surprised. Vanessa grinned. "And that's why we call you Sidewinder. You come at problems sideways."

Isabelle piped up. "Is there a heat sensor inside the case?"

"Not to my knowledge," Greg replied.

Misty handed the welding torch to Aleesha. "You're the surgeon. You do the honors."

Aleesha rolled her eyes. "Everybody stand back from the patient. I never did like being hovered over in the operating room."

Misty watched her colleague's deft touch as she used the very tip of the blue flame to cut through the computer's thin metal skin. In a few minutes, Aleesha lifted away most of the side of the box and stood back.

Everybody took turns peering inside. Misty spotted the

unusually large hard drive case right away. It was vacuum-sealed, and Greg assured them any attempt to cut open the device would result in the acid foam being fired and the hard drive being destroyed.

Misty commented, "I don't mean to be dense here, but why don't we just try your password? Even Russians enter their passwords incorrectly now and then. There has to be a provision to re-enter a password if the first try doesn't work."

Aleesha stared doubtfully at the hermetically sealed hard drive and nodded. "I say we try it. I can stand by with the torch to rip the box open and flush off the foam, but I couldn't save the whole drive."

Katrina, the team's sniper and famously steady of hand, was assigned to take care of any foam once Aleesha sliced the hard drive open. The two women took a few minutes to get into position, then they nodded at Greg. Misty held her breath as he plugged the computer into the voltage regulator he'd set up while the others were getting ready for the possible emergency surgery.

He turned on the computer.

A green light illuminated on the front panel, and the hard drive whirred as it spun up to operating speed. So far so good.

"Here goes," Greg announced.

Misty watched on the monitor they'd attached while Greg typed in the command to open his database. The main operating program loaded like a charm and the Cyrillic welcome screen popped up. That was good news at any rate. The computer had been through an explosion, a couple of rough chases, and some extreme temperature changes in the past several days.

"Ready, ladies?" Greg asked quietly.

"Go for it," Aleesha murmured.

Greg typed in the name of his data file, *Igra konstayah.* Misty translated the Russian in her head. End Game. Interesting choice. What was this the end of? A gambit of some kind, but for whom?

Aleesha bent down close to the hard drive to listen more closely. Nodded up at Greg.

He typed in the password, a long string of random letters and numbers. Checked it twice. Nodded grimly. "Here goes."

He hit Enter.

The hard drive spun.

A red light, indicating the hard drive was in use, flashed.

And the database opened.

Misty exhaled hard. Thank God.

Greg sagged in relief beside her.

Jack held out a small plastic gizmo. "This is a portable hard drive. It'll hold 200 gigabytes of information. Will that cover your database?"

Greg nodded. "It's mostly text. It has some pictures and drawings in it, though."

Misty remarked, "Well let's make a copy of it, for God's sake, so we don't have to go through this again to open the darned thing."

Greg grinned up at her. "I dunno. The past couple of days have been pretty exciting."

She glared at him in mock anger. He laughed and plugged the portable drive into a USB port on the computer's back side. He typed in a copy command.

"Problem," Aleesha announced, her ear still plastered to the hard drive case. "Something just clicked."

The red light on the front of the computer flickered, indicating that a file transfer was in progress. A corresponding blue light lit up on the portable drive.

"The file's copying now," Greg bit out.

"Another click," Aleesha announced. "Sounds like some sort of countdown timer."

"Is there another command? An abort command you can give the computer?" Misty asked urgently.

Greg replied, "No! But it's still copying."

Aleesha said tersely, "I'm betting three's the magic number. Get ready to spray, Cobra. If this thing clicks again, we're going in. I'm going to slash the sides open with the torch and rip the top off. It'll happen fast. A few seconds. Start spraying for all you're worth when I say 'go.'" Aleesha turned on the torch and held it ready.

Another second ticked by. And another. The lights continued to flicker as the precious files were copied. C'mon, c'mon. How long could one file take to copy?

"Three clicks!" Aleesha burst out. She ran the torch down one side of the metal case and started across the top of it with her right hand. Simultaneously with her left hand, she was already wedging a pair of pliers into the gap and tearing at the case.

"Go!" Aleesha ordered.

Kat contorted herself almost sideways to aim at the narrow gap opening up under Aleesha's hands. She shot a heavy spray of water inside the drive. The device made a horrible screeching noise. Aleesha finished ripping the side of the case, and Kat drenched the interior. Flecks of white foam floated out of the mangled metal box. The lights on the front of the computer flickered. Went out.

After a minute or so, Aleesha and Kat straightened up.

Into the heavy silence, Misty commented, "I think the patient's dead, Doctor."

Everyone laughed.

Misty said quietly, "Yeah, but did we get the data off the drive before it died?"

Greg looked around the room. "Only one way to find out. Anybody got a computer? A working one?"

Chapter 14

Misty sat back from the computer screen, stretching her arms up over her head. Warm hands landed on her shoulders, massaging them with enough force to make her groan with pleasure.

"You need to take a break," Greg murmured.

"I'm almost done translating the Medusa report you gave me, and General Wittenauer wants it right away."

"Have you figured out who the informant was yet?" he asked quietly.

"I think Vanessa was right. Based on what's in here, I'm guessing it was someone in the Pentagon who was involved with sanitizing our personnel files and personal histories when we became special operators."

"Take a walk with me."

"But the report—"

"Will wait a few minutes. We've been working for hours."

She smiled up at him. "You're right."

"There's something I want to show you."

Intrigued, she let him lead her toward the back of the house. He opened a glass French door and held it open for her. She stepped outside and was immediately assaulted by a strong, cold wind. And it smelled of the ocean, wild and stormy. She took a long, deep breath of it.

"There's more. But you'll need this." He held out a yellow rubber rain slicker.

"It's not raining." Nonetheless, she shrugged it on while he donned a matching slicker.

"This way. Watch your step. It's slippery."

He led her to the edge of the clifftop terrace and then appeared to step off the edge. She rushed over to where he disappeared and grinned in surprise. A narrow stone staircase was carved right out of the cliff and it wound down toward the waves crashing onto the rocks below. *He remembered.* She'd told him once that she loved the combination of ocean and rocky cliffs.

She hurried down the stone steps after him, and before long saw what he meant about them being slippery. Salt spray from below wetted the steps and stone balustrade until she was forced to slow down. She turned a hairpin corner and smiled broadly. A small terrace perched here, a pair of curving teak chaises inviting a person to sit and take in nature's glory. The terrace had a glass wall facing the sea. With the exception of droplets of spray on the glass, the view was unimpeded.

"Tide's coming in," he commented.

The waves below rolled and crashed, rolled and crashed again. A gust of wind carried a burst of spray up to coat their faces and hands.

"Feels like a storm's coming," she remarked. She sat

down beside him. He reached across the narrow gap and captured her hand, linking their fingers together. They sat there for a while, and Misty reveled in the power and wildness of the seething ocean reaching up toward them as if frustrated at its inability to suck them in.

Finally, Misty asked, "Any luck determining if you got all your files or not?"

"I'm not sure. Something's funny about the files, but I haven't put my finger on what's missing, yet. But I did retrieve most of them. Certainly enough to trade for my safety for a while at least."

"From whom?"

He stared out to sea and didn't even acknowledge her question. Although, truth be told, she knew whom. The Russian and American governments.

A fine, gray mist began to fall, mingling with the spray from below as the tide climbed over the rocks and started up the cliff face toward them.

"Let's go back in," he suggested. "We're getting soaked out here."

The climb back up the cliff was treacherous. They ended up climbing side-by-side, he hanging onto the balustrade and she balancing herself against the rough cliff face. By the time they struggled to the top rain was falling in cold, sharp sheets, stinging their faces and driving inside their hoods uncomfortably.

As Greg closed the patio door behind them, shutting out the storm, he laughed ruefully. "And to think I was hoping to watch the sunset with you."

"I'll take a storm rolling in any day over some smarmy sunset."

He smiled down at her. "How about a hot shower to warm you up?"

She glanced around. They were alone. "Join me?"

His eyes lit up. "Are you sure?"

She nodded and smiled.

"I don't need two invitations for that," he murmured under his breath as Vanessa came into the room. Misty's frozen toes curled in delight.

"You two look like drowned rats!" Vanessa exclaimed.

Misty laughed. "I feel like one, too. We took a walk to work out the kinks and a storm caught us."

Vanessa shook her head. "I knew you liked water, Misty, but I thought you meant warm beaches and climates."

"I usually do. And speaking of warm, I think I'm going to go take a hot shower." She headed for the wing of guest suites. As she reached the stairs, she threw a significant glance over her shoulder at Greg. He smiled and nodded fractionally.

Greg watched Misty go until Vanessa cleared her throat—loudly—behind him. He turned to face her.

"You like her, don't you?" Vanessa asked.

"What's not to like?"

"She hasn't always had an easy time with men, you know."

He nodded. "She's talked to me about that. Apparently, some men have trouble looking past her more obvious physical attributes. Which is their loss. She's an extraordinary woman."

Vanessa leveled a steady look at him. "She is, indeed. And that's why I'd hate to see her get hurt."

Greg cocked an eyebrow. "Are you asking me my intentions toward her or warning me off her, Major?"

"Which should I be doing?"

"Neither. I'm not out to hurt her. If anything, she's the one playing coy with me. I'm more than willing to commit to a relationship with her."

"Then why aren't you together?"

He pursed his lips. "Because you're talking to me and keeping me from joining her in the shower."

Vanessa laughed. "Deal with it. You two will have plenty of time with each other later." The smile faded from her face. "Misty gives her heart cautiously, but once she's committed to something or someone, she goes all the way. So I have to wonder…what's holding her back from committing all the way to you?"

"Who says she hasn't committed to me?"

It was Vanessa's turn to purse her lips. "I've been to hell and back with Misty a couple times already. I know her very well. And she's holding out on you."

Greg crossed his arms. "What do you suggest I do about it?"

"Fix the problem. Whatever you're doing or not doing that's making her cautious…fix it."

"I sense a threat hanging at the end of that sentence."

"No threat, Gregorii. Just don't hurt my Misty. Or you'll have all the Medusas to deal with. We take care of our own."

"And I take care of my own as well. I'm working as quickly as I can so she and I can be together for as long as she wants me."

"What's keeping you apart?"

"With all due respect, Major, don't you think that's between Misty and me?"

The American woman sighed. "You're probably right. Just don't let her down, will you? She's taken a big chance on you."

Greg nodded. He turned to head upstairs, but damned if General Wittenauer didn't choose that very moment to step into the living room.

The older man said jovially, "Just the man I was hoping to see. Perhaps I could have a moment of your time."

Greg sighed. That hot shower with Misty was becoming less and less of a possibility. "Let me guess. You want to interrogate me regarding my intentions toward Captain Cordell."

The man had the grace to look startled for a moment. "As a matter of fact, that is something I'd like to discuss with you."

So much for the steamy shower with Misty. Damn. "Go ahead. Tell me how if I break her heart I'll have you to answer to as well as her." He nodded his head toward Vanessa.

Wittenauer laughed and looked back and forth between him and Vanessa. "Did Viper already read you the riot act?"

Greg nodded.

"Excellent. Then I can move on immediately to mentioning my past as a Special Forces operator and how I still know a thing or two about eliminating people when they least expect it."

Greg grinned. "I wouldn't expect any less of you, sir."

"Outstanding. So. Tell me how you're coming with your database. What's in it that you're so fired up to recover?"

Great. He'd got to move on from dancing around threats of bodily harm if he messed up things with Misty to dancing around uncomfortable questions he wasn't yet ready to answer. Not until he knew for sure the whole database had been recovered. If he had the whole thing, then he'd be in a position to bargain for a real and lasting truce with both governments. If he only had part of it, he'd have to hope he got the most vital bits—the ones that each respective government would pay big currency—in cash or favors—to get their hands on.

Wittenauer was still pressing him for details on the MiG he'd flown out of Russia and how he'd managed to steal the damned thing when Misty came down the stairs. She looked rosy and warm—and seduceable, dammit!

She took one look at Vanessa and Wittenauer grilling him and a wide grin spread across her face. She rolled her eyes at him behind their backs and then stepped into the room.

She interjected gently, "You know, if you two would lay off him long enough for us to get back to work, I might have the Medusa report translated for you in the next hour or so, and Greg just might have some of those answers you're looking for."

Greg's tormentors took the hint, and in short order, Misty and Greg were alone in the computer lab.

He gathered her up in his arms with a groan. "If this room weren't so incredibly sterile and brightly lit, I'd make love to you right here, right now."

She buried her face against his neck, mumbling, "The down side of having a big, interfering family. They kill a girl's love life."

"They're just looking out for you," he replied. "Let's kill off these computer projects and go to bed early tonight. We'll lock the door and turn off our phones and they'll have to leave us alone."

She leaned back to smile up at him. "Deal. But kiss me to seal it."

He took her face in both hands. "God, you're beauti-

at softball. I hit like a girl, catch like a girl, throw like a girl, and for some reason when I'm on a softball field, I run like a girl. I suck at it."

"Thank God. I was beginning to worry you were perfect."

She laughed up at him. "Well, if it's perfection you're looking to debunk, I hate making my bed and hanging up clothes, too."

"But I bet you do both."

"Well, yes. Otherwise my room would get too messy to find anything."

"Like I said. Perfect."

She stuck her tongue out at him and went back to typing.

"What are you doing?" he asked.

"Giving the operating system directions to separate out the database code from any other type of embedded code. Once it's done that, we ought to be able to take a look at the underlying data and see what it is."

"I don't care what it is. I just want it out of there."

She nodded absently, typing in another long string of command language. Then she hit the enter key and leaned back.

"Do we have enough time to fool around while it sorts everything out?"

She grinned up at him. "Sorry. This mini-computer is wicked fast. It'll have the data sorted in—" A beep from the computer interrupted her. "—that long."

He leaned over her shoulder to see what they had.

"Aha! This is a graphics data set!" she exclaimed after a few seconds. "In my last air force tour, I was a test pilot for a new training-jet prototype. The schematics the engineers created looked like this."

"Can you reconstitute the pictures?"

"I think I saw a graphic program on this system when it booted up. Lemme check."

In a minute, she had the high-powered graphic art design program open and was loading the raw data into it. Within ten minutes or so, she was ready to run a graphic depiction of the data. In other words, she was ready to turn all the zeros and ones into pictures. She hit Enter.

The picture started forming at the top of the screen and built slowly in horizontal rows, inch by inch down the screen. By about three inches down the screen, a sick feeling was beginning to form in the pit of his stomach.

"Is there any way to tell when or how this data got put on my computer?" he asked through the bile backing up in his throat.

"There may be a time-date group with it. Once this drawing is done, I'll take a look."

But by the time the picture was half-drawn, he knew. He didn't need her to look. Anatoly had commented about giving Vasily a parting gift before he defected. Greg had assumed the tech meant the secure computer and its encrypted database. He'd never dreamed Anatoly had put something else on the hard drive. Especially not this.

Damn, damn, damn. *Not this!*

Chapter 15

Misty started. Stared at the complex drawing on the screen in front of her. She knew those lines. Recognized the wiring diagram in front of her. She exclaimed, "This is an airplane schematic!" She glanced up at Greg, noting that he looked faintly gray. Must be the bright fluorescent lighting washing out his skin tones.

"You never told me you brought out the blueprints for the jet you stole, too!"

He shrugged but said nothing.

"General Wittenauer will be thrilled. When the MiG blew up, everyone who'd wanted to get a look at the new plane was devastated. But this is just as good. Better, maybe. This will save the American government months of drawing up their own schematics of the jet. The engineers can feed these to the computers and be running flight simulations in a matter of a few days. This is awesome!"

She stood up and gave him an enthusiastic hug. "Let's go tell General Wittenauer."

"You go on ahead and give him the good news. I want to make a few more copies of my database and shut it down. I'll be up in a minute."

She nodded and headed upstairs. The smell of steak pulled her up the steps and toward the kitchen in the middle of the house. The men were cooking supper. Fortunately, Dexter Thorpe, Isabelle's significant other, looked as though he knew what he was doing. There seemed to be some cooking crisis in progress, however, because Dex was barking out orders in rapid-fire succession at the moment. She sat down at a barstool and enjoyed the show until the flurry of activity settled back down to a marginally sane level.

She was just opening her mouth to tell the general her good news when the overhead lights went out. All the power went out, in fact. Which meant that, situated on an isolated cliff like this on a stormy night, the house went pitch-black. As special operators they knew what to do: they all froze in place. General Wittenauer, the ranking officer present, called for a check-off, and everyone within earshot of him took turns reporting their current position.

A voice called down from upstairs. "All the Medusas except Sidewinder are with me at the top of the stairs and fully loaded." That meant they all were carrying loaded weapons with the safeties off. "Are we clear to descend?"

"Take command, Scat," the general said briskly. Which made sense. Jack was currently a field operative and Delta team commander. General Wittenauer drove a desk most of the time these days.

Jack called back to Vanessa, "Sidewinder's with us. We're in the kitchen and loaded."

Misty responded, "I'm not packing. Greg's last known position is the computer room."

Jack swore under his breath, then called, "Medusas. Go get him. My team is heading outside to sweep the grounds. Keep your fire directed away from windows."

Misty clenched her jaw grimly. Fields of fire were the directions in which bullets flew. If Jack was talking about controlling fire, he thought someone had cut the power from outside preparatory to an assault on the house. Her gut tightened sharply. His logic was sound.

"Sidewinder. Join the Medusas."

That was Jack.

"Roger. I'm moving."

Someone was trying to kill Greg. Fear and fury mingled unpleasantly on the back of her tongue. She swallowed both, allowing herself to feel only grim determination to keep him safe at all costs. She was *not* losing him after all they'd gone through together! She headed across the living room quickly, picturing the locations of furniture in her head. She banged her shin on the corner of a coffee table she misjudged, but in a few seconds, she stood at the top of the stairs leading down to the lower level.

"Sidewinder?" Vanessa murmured.

"Here."

"Take my sidearm."

Misty held out a hand, and the sureness with which Viper laid the weapon in her palm made her ask, "You ladies got your night eyes on?"

"Yup."

"Damn, it's dark in here without them," Misty responded. "I'm walking blind."

"Take my arm," Aleesha said from close by. Misty

reached out, and her teammate took her hand and guided it under her elbow.

"Stairs," Aleesha murmured.

Misty groped for the rail and was able to move downward quickly with its assistance.

"Across the billiards room now."

Misty felt the transition from hardwood floor to carpet as they passed the pool table and reached the home theater. Only twenty more feet or so to the computer room.

"Door's closed," Aleesha announced.

Misty snorted. "It had better be locked, too, or I'll have to beat him up."

Vanessa spoke ahead of them. "Yup. Locked. You call through the door, Sidewinder. He trusts you."

God, she hoped so.

"Door. Twelve o'clock. Two feet," Aleesha murmured.

Misty reached out and touched the wood panel. "Greg? You in there? It's me."

His voice came out muffled. "Are we under attack?"

"We don't know. Maybe. The guys are outside having a look around and the Medusas are here with me. We're here to collect you and take you back upstairs."

"Why don't I just stay here? There are no outside windows or doors."

"It is a defensible position, but there are no escape routes. We'd rather place you somewhere that gives us a few options for moving you if it gets too hot. Besides, we're not even sure this is an attack. Lightning could have struck a transformer and simply knocked out the power."

The door lock rattled. She heard a faint squeak—the door opening.

Vanessa's disembodied voice came from nearby. "We're wearing night-vision goggles, Greg, and can see perfectly well. We're going to surround you and move you up the stairs. Just flow with us, okay?"

He commented dryly, "Let me guess. You're trained bodyguards, too."

"That's correct," Vanessa replied briskly.

Misty grinned. Poor guy. He was having a hard time adapting to just how macho the Medusas truly were. Aleesha gave her a push, and Misty stumbled forward. She promptly bumped into a familiar form, tall and hard and strong.

"Hey, handsome," she murmured.

"Fancy meeting you like this," he commented back lightly with a fake British accent.

"Shall we go for a stroll?" Misty quipped.

"Love to. After you, my dear."

The Medusas surrounded them and the whole cluster of bodies shuffled back the way they'd come. At the foot of the stairs, Vanessa called out quietly, "Is the field clear at Alpha One?"

In sniper speak, that was the designation of the northernmost and easternmost room in the house…also known as the living room.

No answer from upstairs.

"The boys must still playing cowboys and Indians outside," Misty murmured.

"Let's move," Vanessa ordered.

They climbed the stairs without incident. And then the waiting began. With the forced inactivity, she had far too much time to imagine the worst. This wasn't a problem she'd ever encountered on a mission before. Usually in the down times she envisioned herself cloud-busting in a hot jet or lying on a tropical beach. But visions of Greg, hurt and bleeding, dying even, kept creeping into her brain.

And with each image, awareness pressed more insistently against the walls of her consciousness that she cared for him. Deeply. Very deeply.

Dammit, she was head over heels for the guy.

And she was scared to death he might get hurt or worse.

She fought back her feelings, seeking the calm, cool detachment her line of work required. Yeah, right. So not happening.

As the silence and the darkness dragged on, she clawed her way by inches toward a modicum of calm. Eventually she felt functional, even if she wasn't anywhere near full strength. Her eyes adapted to the deep gloom, and she began to make out the shapes of furniture and her teammates. She sat beside Greg on the living room sofa, which was placed against an interior wall. Katrina and Isabelle manned the windows, peeking out from around the closed curtains.

Vanessa went upstairs and came back with an armload of…something. She stopped in front of Misty. "Here, Sidewinder. A little present for you."

A heavy pile of cloth and wire—and weapons, thank heavens—landed in her lap. "Hallelujah!" she exclaimed, "I've felt naked since this whole thing began."

Greg mumbled, "I wish."

She grinned and batted at his upper arm. "Behave yourself. There are ladies present."

He chuckled as she quickly ran the wires for her throat mike down her shirt and hooked the battery pack on her waistband. She donned her equipment vest and holster, sighing in relief. Now she had the tools of a special operator at hand. And those represented options for her. She subsided on the couch once more, and Greg's arm slid off the back of the couch and around her shoulder.

"Gee," he commented. "You're about as cuddly as a Bradley tank."

"It's a Bradley Fighting Vehicle," she corrected dryly.

He laughed. "And to think—I found a woman who knows the difference."

"That's me. Chock full of fun little surprises like that." She added casually, "I guess that's why we're a match made in heaven. You have your secrets and I have mine."

Greg's arm abruptly went stiff across the back of her back. Tough. Before their relationship went too much farther, he *was* going to have to climb off the fence.

Misty's earbud crackled, "Movement. Six o'clock, forty meters."

She started. That was Dex. He was a longtime Delta operator and a cool customer. Not the kind of guy prone to panic at the sight of a raccoon.

"Say type target," Jack bit out.

"Human. Furtive."

Misty's gut clenched. He sounded awfully darn sure of himself. The fear that had been nipping at her heels ever since they'd left Alaska intensified abruptly. Whoever was chasing Greg was bloody persistent and damned near uncanny at staying on their tails. She was roundly sick of how these hostiles kept turning up practically on top of them.

Jack instructed, "Assume he's hostile, men. Sweep left."

As the team outside crept around to the left flank of their target, Isabelle moved fast across the living room to the foyer on the southeast corner of the main floor and peered out the long window by the front door. She had extraordinary eyesight and was a trained spotter. "IR scope," Isabelle muttered tersely into her throat mike.

Misty knew from experience that Adder's concentration was intense when she was on the job. Katrina moved across the room and laid an infrared night-vision scope in Isabelle's outstretched hand while the spotter never took her eyes off the scene outside.

After a short time, Isabelle murmured, "Sixteen meters to your right, Scat. Twenty meters straight on, Michael."

Bingo. Adder had spotted the hostile and was now vectoring the men in on the target. Misty waited tensely on the couch. Nobody must harm Greg! She realized she was as tight as a spring, ready to throw herself across Greg— to sacrifice her body to save him—at the slightest hint of trouble. She tried to relax, but it was hopeless. She was wound too tight to let it go.

Greg leaned over and asked quietly, "What's going on? Everyone's tense all of a sudden."

She'd forgotten he didn't have an earpiece. "Our guys saw someone and have gone to have a look. Isabelle has spotted the intruder and is guiding the guys to him."

Greg's arm fell away from her and anxiety poured off of him.

She shrugged. "Don't worry. They'll nab the guy. Our team is the best of the best. You'll be perfectly safe."

"I'm worried about you, dammit, not me. I know you. You'll charge out with guns blazing where angels fear to tread. If it gets ugly out there, how am I going to keep you safe?"

She stared over at him in the dark. Unfortunately, all she could make out were shadows upon shadows where his face should be. "I'll be fine. No need to worry about me."

"But I do worry, dammit. I can't help it."

She reached out and touched the black, smooth plane

of his cheek with her fingertips. She breathed, "I know the feeling."

His fingers touched her hand. Tangled with her fingers. Squeezed with silent urgency. And with each passing moment, her heart expanded.

All of a sudden, her earpiece erupted with noise, Jack and the others calling back and forth in rapid-fire succession. As best as Misty could make out, the guys had taken down one hostile and spotted another who'd taken off running. Dex and Michael were giving chase.

The Medusas listened intently but stayed completely quiet, not cluttering up the frequency. The silence outside stretched out into three minutes. Five minutes. Misty's curiosity all but choked her. *What was happening out there?*

Then Dex panted, "Got him."

Jack ordered, "Report."

"When we caught him and tackled him, he pulled a knife. I dropped him."

"Is he dead, or can he be questioned?"

"Sorry. He was good with a knife. I had to kill him."

Isabelle and Kat were dispatched outdoors to help the men clear the area of any further hostiles, and in about a half hour, Jack gave the all clear. Then he startled Misty by saying, "Sidewinder, I need you to bring your friend out here."

"What for?" Misty blurted. It was unusual in the extreme to move a protectee out from under safe cover, particularly so soon after a threat to his life.

"There's something I need him to see."

Misty stood up. "Come with me, Greg. Jack wants to show you something."

He frowned, but stood up. She never got tired of watching his casual grace. He gestured gallantly for her to go first and she smiled up at him. Vanessa, Karen and Aleesha fell in around them, and they all went outside.

Jack called out low, "Over here."

They headed toward a stand of pine trees shrouded in shadows. The rain had mostly stopped for the moment and only a fine, cold drizzle still fell. General Wittenauer and Jack led them deeper into the woods. Their feet moved silently across the sodden pine needles, and for several minutes the only sound was of water dripping through the trees.

And then Misty spied a pair of dark shapes underneath the drooping boughs of a giant white pine. A third dark shape lay at their feet. The group stopped in front of the pair of men.

"Give me your first impression," Jack said to Greg quietly.

"Of what?"

"Of him."

Misty looked down. The black thing at their feet was a body. Wearing a utility vest and radio headset such as she might use. She glanced at the weapon lying beside him…a KEDR machine pistol. Her gaze snapped to his other gear—a PSS silent pistol in a modified quick draw holster and an NRS field knife still clutched in his dead hand.

Was this guy…

"Spetznatz," Greg announced matter-of-factly.

The word thudded like a lump of lead in mud. Misty gaped at him. Spetznatz? As in Russian Special Forces troops? How in the heck did *they* get here?

General Wittenauer said sharply, "And they're hunting you why?"

Misty piped up. "Let's take this conversation back inside. I was about to tell you when the power went out.

Greg and I made a discovery on his computer. We found the blueprints for the prototype MiG he flew out."

"I didn't know I had it." Greg added quickly, "I swear."

Wittenauer muttered something that sounded like *son-ofagun*. Aloud, he said, "This I have to see."

They retreated to the house, and Michael and Dex took the first shift patrolling outside while the others regrouped to plan their next move. Wittenauer cranked up Vanessa's laptop, onto which Misty had already loaded the blue-prints. While the general pored over the drawings, the others got down to the business of defending themselves from any further incursions.

They discussed leaving the premises. After all, the Spetznatz guy they'd killed had both a radio and a cell phone on him. And where there was one of those guys, there were usually several more. The flip side of that coin was that the lone spotter could also have let himself be seen, either as bait to draw them out and test their strength, or to convince them to run.

Eventually, they decided that any Spetznatz team at-tempting to assault this place wouldn't count on the equiv-alent of two full Special Forces units being inside, or upon the fact that the entire house was built of concrete and bul-letproof glass. Plus, the Medusas and company knew the lay of the land, especially after the past hour of running around in the woods.

Jack gave the Medusas a complete briefing on the terrain and vegetation features around the house. They ul-timately agreed it was better to make their stand here, on well-defended home turf, than to end up running around the woods in a free-for-all with a bunch of Russian Special Forces types.

Vanessa laid out a defense plan in case of attack and

assigned firing posts to each of them. Additionally, she put all of them except Misty on a watch rotation. To her, Vanessa said—with a straight face, no less— "I need you to sleep with Greg tonight. Stick to him like glue."

As the others smirked, Greg grinned openly. Misty rolled her eyes. She knew better than to respond to that and open herself up to further comments.

With no lights and no power, it made no sense to stay up any later, and as soon as the ops plan was worked out, Greg murmured to her, "You tired?"

She shrugged. "I'm on guard duty tonight. You go to bed whenever you want to. I'm just here to tag along and keep you alive."

Greg said good night to everyone and headed upstairs with Misty in tow. He stepped into his room and held the door for her.

"I'll park out here," she said.

"I distinctly heard Viper order you to sleep with me."

"She meant that I should guard you while you slept. It's standard procedure in high-threat situations."

Greg's teeth gleamed in a smile. "Do I need to go ask her for a clarification?"

She huffed. "Fine. I'll stand guard inside."

She stepped into the room. He closed the door behind her, and the room went black. They were alone. Finally. And safe for now. Her pent-up tension from the past several days drained away, leaving behind the same rush at being alive that she always got at the end of a successful mission. As she stood there in the dark appreciating the simple act of breathing, she learned something new about being a Special Operator. Victory over death and danger was a hell of an aphrodisiac.

"Misty," he murmured. "You're burning me up, here."

"I'm not even touching you!"

"It's pouring off you like lava off the side of a volcano."

She didn't need to ask what *it* was. *It* was roaring through her, setting her blood on fire and gnawing through her gut with a sexual need so intense she could barely restrain herself from leaping on Greg and ravishing him.

Fingertips touched her cheek, and she jumped.

"Are you sure about this? About us?" he murmured.

She reached up and gripped his wrist to still his hand, which had roamed down to her neck. His other hand came up behind her, tracing the small of her back.

"The only thing I'm sure about right now is that I'm working, and you need to back off."

He stepped so close she felt his chest rising and falling millimeters from hers. "The way I heard it, you're supposed to stick to me like glue." His mouth brushed across her cheekbone.

Her knees started to feel distinctly weak.

He whispered into her hair, "I'm sorry I've put you and your friends in danger."

Her hands crept around his hard waist. "It's our job."

"And you do it so well." He kissed her eyelids gently, and the weak feeling spread down to her toes and up to her belly.

"We can't do this." She sighed.

"I know." His hand speared into her hair, cupping the back of her head. "I also know I can't get enough of you."

Beneath her fingers, his shirt worked free of his pants. As always, the heat of him scalded her. Made her crave more of his skin.

"I really…uhh…have to…uhh…get back to work."

"Right. At being glue." And then his mouth was on hers, and the only thing she could think of was crawling inside him and burying herself in his fire. He backed away from the wall, drawing her with him. She could've torn away. Should've torn away. But damned if she didn't take a step, and then another, seeking his body against hers, following the lure of his mouth, his hands, the mesmerizing attraction that bound her to him more surely than any rope.

He bumped into something and paused, then with a quick stoop and an arm around her thighs, picked her up. Misty started. She wasn't the kind of woman men picked up and carried around, thank you very much. She was a trained killer, for goodness sake.

But then he lowered her to the bed and followed her down, blanketing her in muscle and fire, and she became Woman—not a soldier, not a killer, not a Barbie-doll blonde. Just Woman. How he stripped away all those other layers of her to reveal this core she didn't even know she had, she had no idea. But then he moved against her, and recognition of Man exploded within her. She needed nothing more, wanted nothing more than this moment. Right here, right now.

The cold-edged darkness went soft and warm, words of whispered need swirling around them, gathering them up in an elemental embrace. The night's blanket draped over them as they strained toward one another. She rose to meet him as he sank down, down into her arms and into her soul.

The magic was right there. Same as before. No, better than before. For, this time, at that infinite and momentary pause just before climax, he looked deep into her eyes and whispered, "I love you."

"I love you, too."

For an instant, fear galvanized her. She couldn't believe

she'd just said that! But then, she couldn't believe she'd just heard it, either.

They'd moved together one last time, stirring the fire into a sudden explosion that threw sparks outward to every fiber of her being. She cried aloud, and he leaned down to capture her bliss in his mouth. She surged against him, crying out again and again as the moment rolled on and on through her and left her shuddering in his arms.

She regained awareness of her surroundings slowly. First, his chest against her cheek. Then the silky, short hair at the back of his neck beneath her fingers. The hard thudding of his heart gradually calming beneath her ear. She tilted her head back and tugged him down to her. He obliged and kissed her lingeringly.

"I've missed you so much," she murmured against his mouth.

"I've been right here the whole time," he replied against her lips.

"But that doesn't mean I've given myself permission to have you."

"What do I have to do for you to let go? What is it you need from me?"

"I need you to choose sides. Once and for all."

He pulled back. A sigh brushed her temple. "You want more than that. You want me to choose your side. What if I say I'll cast my lot with the Russians?"

"Then I'll say you're crazy. We just killed a Spetznatz operative out there. The Russians are trying to *kill* you."

He said nothing.

The fog of their lovemaking lifted a bit more, and as they lounged lazily in the afterglow, it occurred to her to wonder just how in the world those Russians had found this place so quickly and with such unerring accuracy. The

Medusas had gone over their step van with a fine-toothed comb. There was absolutely, positively not a tracking device of any kind on it. And they'd just as certainly ditched their Russian tails at the U.S. border earlier. How then? It was almost as if someone had called and told them where the Americans would be….

The chill started at her toes. It worked its way up past her knees to the base of her spine and rattled higher until her throat froze shut with it. Icicles pierced her skull and she nearly cried aloud with the agony of her realization.

"You called them didn't you?"

Greg stared down at her in the darkness, horrified.

And she knew. She *knew* she was right.

She raised herself up on her elbows and stared down at him. She said grimly, "You sonofabitch. You betrayed me. *You betrayed us all.*"

Chapter 16

Invigorated, General Karkarov finished getting dressed. Nothing like an hour or two in a sauna to get the blood flowing.

Gennady hurried up to him, looking more frazzled than usual. "Thank God. There you are, sir! I've been looking all over for you. There's a crisis and you have to answer your telephone right away!"

Gennady was calling it a crisis? Ye gods, the end of the world must be upon them. "What is it?" Karkarov bit out, reaching into the breast pocket of his coat for his cell phone.

Gennady took a look around the changing room. This bath house was reserved for the highest level members of the government and was deserted at the moment. He lowered his voice. "The team you spoke with last night. They've had a…development…and need instructions."

"What the hell do they need to talk to me for? They have their orders. They're supposed to be able to work independently. Give them a job, then hands off and let them do it. That's what their commanders are always railing about."

Gennady shrugged. "Just call them."

The general hit the redial button from the first time the Spetznatz team had contacted him for permission to kill Nemorov.

"Da?" a man said at the other end of the line.

"This is General Karkarov. What has happened?"

"The target called us approximately two hours ago."

"He *what?*"

"A call from Vasily Nemorov was patched through to us from our Command Center—"

Karkarov interrupted, "What the hell did he want?"

"He told us where he was and ordered us not to strike the house because he's inside. In particular, he ordered us to stay down while he arranged for it to look like a strike. In the meantime, he's destroyed every computer in the place before power or telephone service would be restored."

"Why? Did he say?"

"He said he'd just discovered drawings of some kind on a computer he has with him. He says the computer came out of his ride to America. He's doing his best to find and destroy all copies that might have been made of the schematics."

Karkarov's jaw sagged. Schematics? *The MiG.* Somebody had put a set of the jet's schematics on the plane's computer? He'd have the traitor executed when he found him. And Vasily was calling his own assassins to order them to take out the computer and the schematics? *Did I misjudge Vasily after all?*

"What are your orders, sir?"

"Have you verified he's at the location he gave you?"

"Affirmative. We spotted the target along with several other individuals inside the house before the power went out."

"We can't trust Vasily. Can you take out all the computers?"

"We'll either have to break into the house or torch it. And yes, both are possible."

"You decide which option is best. But destroy all the computers that might hold copies of the drawings he mentioned."

"And our previous orders? Are they still a go? Do we kill Nemorov, too?"

Karkarov hesitated. And then went with his gut. "No. I think I should like to speak to the good colonel before he meets his end. There will be time enough later to kill him if we must."

"Very well. We will stand down on killing Nemorov and shift target to the house and its computers."

"Keep me informed as you have time. I want a full report the moment the operation is completed."

"Roger, sir. Will comply."

Greg leaped out of bed after Misty. He knew better than to touch her right now—she'd rip his hand off. "Stop! You have to listen to me!"

She whirled around, naked and glorious in her rage, and glared at him. Her voice was terrible in its contained wrath. "Fine. Talk."

"Discovering those schematics changes everything. If the Russians find out I brought those with me, they'll know for sure I betrayed them. They'll go to the ends of the earth to destroy me. The Russian government has a vengeful streak as wide as the Volga River. I can't hand those drawings over to the Americans. Doing so is a death sentence for me. And yet, knowing they exist, I can't ask you not to hand them over. You're loyal to your country. Sworn to serve and defend it. And you'll do the right thing at all costs."

"What does all of this have to do with you betraying us by calling the Russians?"

He didn't know if the *us* she referred to was him and her, or her and the Medusas. Either way, the accusation was a dagger to the heart…because it was true.

"Misty, when I left Russia, I didn't really care if I lived or died. I knew Karkarov would probably double-cross me. But I didn't care. I just wanted out. And then I met you. You changed the equation. Hell, you broke the equation. After I met you, I started thinking about crazy things like growing old. Like spending my life with you. And that meant I had to live. We both had to live."

Too tense to stand still, he began to pace.

"I figured if I could just get my files out of the computer, I could blackmail Karkarov and the Russians into backing off. Into letting me live. And then you and I could be together. But then you found those damned drawings. As soon as Karkarov realizes I smuggled out the schematics, knowingly or otherwise, he'll be *convinced* I betrayed him. And I'm a dead man."

"What's so important about those schematics? According to you, this Russian general was willing to let the Americans have the whole bloody airplane!"

He turned to face her. "Ahh, but you're wrong. The plan all along was to destroy the plane within a few hours of it landing in Alaska."

Misty frowned. "So, the Americans were to get a

glimpse of the plane. Just enough to know it exists. And then it was to be blown up."

He nodded and held his silence to let her work through the logic for herself.

She looked up at him, startled. "Is there something wrong with the MiG?"

"You tell me. You're the test pilot. You saw the schematics."

She was silent for several moments more. "There's a problem with the aerodynamic stability, isn't there?"

"It's worse than that. Picture the drawings you saw. Then picture the plane you saw."

She frowned a moment longer. And then comprehension broke over her face with the force of religious enlightenment. "It was a fake."

He nodded, encouraging her to continue the logic.

"The jet you flew out of Russia wasn't the same one as in the schematics. It was a mock-up built to look like the stealth jet in the drawings. Are there any actual stealth jets built?"

Bingo. They had a winner. She'd arrived at the $64,000 question.

He answered grimly, "No, there are no jets built from those drawings."

She nodded as the revelations continued to flow. "Of course not. The schematics are fatally flawed. The Russians wouldn't bother building a prototype from them. But they didn't want the U.S. to know that. Your general wanted to fool the Americans into thinking Russia has a fully developed, next-generation stealth program!"

"Exactly. That's why the jet I flew out had to be destroyed immediately. And it's why those schematics are so dangerous. The Russians will go to any lengths to destroy them and see that they're never handed over to the American government. And if I were to hand them over, they'd most certainly destroy me."

She frowned and didn't reply. The loyal American agent balking at not giving her country such a powerful negotiating tool over a rival. He sighed. "Look at it this way. The Russians will never know that an American test pilot got a good look at those drawings. You'll be able to tell the American government all it needs to know—that the next-generation, stealth MiG was a hoax. If those drawings are destroyed now, the Russians will never know how Uncle Sam found that out. But if those schematics are not destroyed…"

She finished for him. "Word will leak out that America got its hands on them. The hoax will be revealed, Russia will get egg on its face, and they'll be looking to take it out on somebody." She stared at him, frustrated. "All right. All right. I see your logic. But to call in a Spetznatz team to attack us? They're deadly. We could still all die."

He shrugged. "I called them to tell them *not* to stage an attack. That I would destroy all of the computers. They agreed, but it looks like they went back on their word."

She pulled on the remainder of her clothes in silence. As her head emerged from a black turtleneck, she asked, "What can you tell me about this Spetznatz team?"

"Not much. I was patched through from their command center. I called from the computer room in the basement when you went upstairs to tell General Wittenauer we'd discovered the schematics."

"Did the Russians knock out the power to the house or did you?"

Man, she's good. Doesn't miss a detail. "I cut the power. I had to keep you from transmitting the file with the drawings in it to anyone. I knew there was rotten cell phone coverage in this area, and I didn't see any wireless Internet servers downstairs, so I figured you'd have to use a phone line or a fax to send out the data."

"The Russians showed up here about an hour after you made the call. The guy Dex killed must've been their initial spotter, then. The rest of the team is probably trying to figure out what the hell happened to their guy and just who they're up against right about now."

"The team leader was stunned when I called him. I wouldn't bet you a kopek that his orders had been anything other than to kill me."

"And after your call to him? What will happen next?"

"The Russian army maintains centralized command and control. The Spetznatz team will have to report in to headquarters, relay my message and request new instructions."

She glanced at her watch. "They've had about an hour to plan their next move. Which will now have to include a move against the house."

She jammed an earpiece into her ear and held the cloth strap of a throat microphone in front of her mouth. She transmitted, "We've got a problem, folks. I can't go into the details right now, but Greg knows the Spetznatz team outside is probably going to make an assault on the house. They're most likely under orders to destroy every computer in the place."

A short silence. Then she said, "Roger. Two minutes."

She looked up. "You've got a minute-and-a-half to get dressed. Warmly. In wool if you've got any. This could be a long night, and wool holds heat when it's wet."

Misty led the way downstairs, still reeling from Greg's revelations. This changed everything about tonight's mission. It wasn't a personnel protection job any more. Now they were facing a full-out assault. She didn't know whether to strangle Greg for making the call or hug him for 'fessing up to it. But right now, she didn't have time to figure it out.

The entire team was assembled in the living room when they arrived, minus Katrina and Dex, who were taking their turns outside on a watch rotation. But both of them were up on radios.

"What's up?" Vanessa asked without preamble.

Misty replied tersely. "It's a long story for later. But Greg cut the power supply and phone lines to the house from downstairs. He called the Spetznatz team outside and told them where to find the house, but not to strike because he would destroy all the computers in it. Obviously his plan backfired. They may or may not still be under orders to kill him."

Jack leaped up off the couch. "And we shouldn't let them kill him why?" he demanded angrily.

"Like I said. A story for later. Greg had good reasons for what he did. What we need to focus on right now is responding to the Spetznatz team outside."

"Do you trust him?" Vanessa asked, her voice hard.

Misty took a deep breath. Looked over at him in the shadows. He looked back at her steadily. Grimly. It had all come down to this. Her call. Was he a good guy or not?

She answered slowly, "I believe he's telling me the truth."

Dodge. Weave. Evade. You chicken! Way to avoid the question. She wanted to believe he was a good guy. Needed to believe he was on her side. But did she know that for sure? Absolutely not.

Vanessa accepted the answer without comment, but

Misty had no doubt she'd caught the fact that Misty hadn't directly answered the question.

After a pause, Vanessa said, "A few of us can pull Greg out of here while the others defend the house."

Greg spoke up quietly. "I don't think they'll let any of us leave. They'll realize you all may take laptops with you. I was clear with them. *All* the computers have to be destroyed."

"What the heck's on our computers that's so important?" Vanessa blurted.

Misty cut in. "Those schematics I told you about. Of the prototype MiG Greg defected with. Russia will go to the wall to keep them from falling into U.S. hands."

Wittenauer interjected, "Why?"

"Part of the long story, sir," Misty replied.

The general nodded and threw Greg a look that promised he'd have the full story, and soon.

Vanessa recapped. "So the guys outside will want to destroy any laptops, portable drives or computer chips we take out with us, too?"

Greg nodded. "Yes—I told them they were all compromised."

Jack burst out, "I can't believe I'm having this conversation. Why haven't you put a bullet through his head, Sidewinder? If you're too emotionally involved with him to do it, I'll pull the damned trigger."

Misty stepped up to him. Jack might have a temper and be capable of breathtaking violence, but she had faith in his ability to control it, even under these circumstances. "Sir," she started. Stopped. "Jack. Trust me on this one. He had a good reason for what he did. Can we focus on what we're going to do now?"

"What do you recommend?" Scatalone bit out.

"I say we give them exactly what they want."

Everyone blinked.

"Let's wire the house to blow up. We'll set up dummies to make it look like we're still inside. We'll booby-trap the heck out of the place with explosives. We slip outside and wait for the Russians to make their assault. First grenade they launch through a window, we blow the house sky-high. They'll think they got a lucky hit, killed everyone inside and wiped out every bit of electronics in the joint."

Silence.

Were they all chewing on her idea, or just too stunned over its stupidity to speak? "Comments?" she asked.

Jack began to chuckle. Then Vanessa. And then everybody joined in.

Wittenauer spoke first. "We're standing in ten million dollars' worth of house."

Misty shrugged. "There's a hundred million dollars' worth of data on Greg's computer."

The general stared hard at her and Greg. Then his mouth curved into a grin. "At least I'm not on the receiving end of the crazy stunt this time. The difficulty will be in sneaking out of here undetected, though."

Vanessa spoke up. "We'll need a distraction. We already have Cobra and Dex outside. They can create some sort of ruckus."

Aleesha chimed in. "The two of them could make a lot of noise. Like a bunch of cops storming the woods."

Misty added, "We could call the local police and get them to drive up to the end of the driveway with a bunch of sirens going."

Nods all around. It could work.

Vanessa asked Greg, "Any guess how soon your boys will make their move?"

"They're not *my* boys," he retorted sharply. "And they'll have to make their hit tonight. They understand they have to complete the mission before power is restored to the house."

Vanessa commented, "We've got to move fast, then. They could strike at any minute. I want all the explosives we've got with us on this table in three minutes. Mamba, you and Michael take a look at the house and figure out how to take this place down."

Aleesha grumbled, "All this concrete? It's a bloody fortress. How about a really big fire instead?"

Vanessa shrugged. "That'll work. Something big and hot, though, so nobody doubts that all occupants and computers inside are dead."

"One flashy fire coming up, boss."

Misty and Greg were tasked to build dummies. They ended up stuffing plastic grocery bags with wadded up newspaper for the heads. They stuffed shirts and pants with newspaper as well, and sacrificed a couple of rifle slings attached to long sticks of firewood to look like weapons.

They taped one dummy to the wall beside a ground-floor window. A careful drape of the curtain to let just a sliver of the dummy's silhouette be visible from outside, and they were on to the next dummy. They scattered the crude, life-sized dolls all over the house. Several sat on the sofas in the living room. One crouched by the back patio door. Another one went in the basement just outside the computer lab as if standing guard.

It took a half hour, but finally all the dummies were in place. Aleesha and Michael were still rigging the house to blow up, so Misty had a quick conversation with Jack, who'd just gotten back inside from rendezvousing with

Katrina to hand over the remote detonator to the explosives.

Then she murmured to Greg, "Come with me."

He followed her upstairs and she led him to Jack and Vanessa's room.

"What're you doing?" he asked curiously.

She rooted around in Jack's rucksack of gear and came up with something that looked like black cloth. "We need to get you suited up in black. Put this over your sweater. Its fibers deflect infrared sensors."

"You're kidding."

"Nope. The armed forces have been busy inventing cool toys since you left the States five years ago."

He rolled his eyes. "You'd be surprised how much of it I was able to keep abreast of, sitting at my desk in the Kremlin."

Vanessa called from downstairs. "We're ready. Let's go."

Greg stepped in front of her quickly and blocked the door. "Misty. I did what I thought was best for the two of us."

She closed her eyes for a pained second. "Later. After this is over."

He nodded grimly and stepped aside.

They headed downstairs to where the rest of the team was assembled, everyone garbed in the same flat black clothing she and Greg wore.

Vanessa said calmly, "Sir, if you'd make the call to the police to let them know we're ready to roll."

Wittenauer nodded and opened his cell phone. He murmured quietly for several seconds, then hung up. "Three minutes. The entire sheriff's department has turned out to enjoy the show. They promise to make a whole hell of a lot of noise."

Vanessa nodded and keyed her microphone. "Cobra, Dex. You're on in three minutes. Are you in position?"

A double click on the radios was all the answer they got. Which meant the two of them had located the Spetznatz team and were in position close to them.

The entire group moved into the kitchen and waited in the shadows not far from the patio door. The seconds ticked by maddeningly slowly. And then, in the distance, Misty heard the faint wail of a siren. And then another. And then so many sirens she could hardly hear the wind and rain pounding against the windows any more.

Dex murmured, "Our targets are on the move. Let's go, Cobra."

Right now, the two of them should be crashing through the woods like a herd of charging bulls, flushing out the Spetznatz team.

Katrina transmitted next. "They're on the run. Headed your way, Dex."

Between the two of them, they forced the Russians to zigzag through the woods, bouncing back and forth between them. The sirens got louder and the squeals of tires split the night.

"If that doesn't have them distracted, I give up," Vanessa breathed. "Let's move."

Jack went first, slipping out the back door into the night. The team fanned out, diving out the door and moving across the patio low and fast. Misty's job was to move Greg down the stairs toward the water. She grabbed his arm and hustled him out the door to the staircase. If possible, the steps were even more slippery than before.

The two of them moved downward fast, following the shadows of Karen, Aleesha and Michael. The tide was out now, and a narrow strand of gravel lined the bottom of the rocky cliff.

As they hit the rolling pebbles, Misty muttered, "Go slow. Quiet is more important than fast."

He nodded his understanding. They eased forward side-by-side.

The darkness was thick, and sheets of rain sliced at her. Her impulse was to duck her head against the cutting water, but she had to keep a sharp lookout. She pulled her night vision goggles down over her eyes as much to keep the water out of them as to see better. The beach leapt into lime-green relief. The team clustered just beyond the point of the nearest cliff, out of sight of the house.

Vanessa and Jack brought up the rear and joined them. "Cobra, Dex. We're clear. As soon as the Russians attack the house, blow it up."

An ominous double click was the only reply.

They didn't have long to wait. The Spetznatz team was hardcore. They'd been given a mission, and they'd die rather than fail. If this had turned into a suicide mission, so be it.

Dex reported, "They're moving. Rushing straight at the house. The assault is commencing."

Vanessa ordered, "Remote-fire the guns, Cobra."

"Roger," Katrina replied.

Jack and Vanessa had rigged up a couple of MP-5s right outside the house to fire on remote controls. It didn't matter where they were aimed. The Russians just needed to hear gunfire. They would believe it was aimed at them regardless of where the bullets actually went.

The rat-a-tat of gunfire erupted.

Dex chuckled. "That got 'em. They're charging the house, full-speed. Any second now, Cobra."

"Standing by," came Katrina's preternaturally calm voice. Misty knew that tone. The sniper had settled into an emotionless, almost zen state of readiness to fire.

From the top of the cliff, they heard the distinctive *whump* of a rocket-propelled grenade firing. Almost instantly, a tremendous explosion rocked the night. Greg grabbed her and shoved her against the cliff wall as stone and scree showered down from above, sheltering her with his body.

And then a second explosion kaboomed. The ground beneath their feet shook and an even bigger rock fall littered the beach a few feet from them. Boulders the size of armchairs fell this time, and Greg smashed her flat against the rocks.

The entire sky lit up orange, and slashes of rain cut through the cloud of smoke beginning to float out over the water.

"Nice explosion," Dex commented dryly. "The place is burning like a torch. I had no idea concrete burned like that."

Aleesha grinned beside Misty and transmitted back, "It doesn't. But natural gas does. We turned on the ovens and burners before we left. That first explosion was the RPG lighting off the gas fumes. It powdered enough flammable bits of the house like the kitchen cabinets and furniture so that when our explosives ignited the dust they lit off everything in the house at once."

"Say status of Spetznatz team," Vanessa ordered.

"Just climbing off their bellies now," Katrina reported. "And if I do say so myself, they're looking a bit stunned that their RPG did all that."

Misty grinned broadly.

A few moments went by, then Dex reported, "They're bugging out."

Vanessa turned to General Wittenauer. "Call the sheriff again. Remind him and his men *not* to engage the Russians. *Let them go.* Not only would they slaughter the police, but we need them to take word of Greg's demise and the destruction of all the computers back to Moscow."

While Wittenauer made the call, Misty sagged in relief against the cliff. They'd done it. The Russians thought Greg was dead and the MiG schematics and his data files destroyed. He was free.

But where did that leave them?

Chapter 17

Greg was cold and wet, but he was mostly numb. They'd done it. Misty and the Medusas had convinced the Russians that he and his computer were utterly and completely destroyed, along with all the intelligence they'd both held. He was free.

They shivered on the beach for over an hour. The stairs going back up the cliff had been wrecked in the explosion, the top fifty feet of them blasted right off the face of the rock. But then a quiet roar captured his attention. It came not from above, but from the sea. A sleek, dark-gray silhouette appeared around the end of the point. It was a big, muscular motorboat with machine guns mounted fore and aft and a half dozen black-clad soldiers manning both vessel and guns.

Two rubber dinghys dropped into the water and separated from the larger fast boat. They zipped ashore and he and the Medusas climbed into them. In short order, they all were aboard the fast boat and strapped down to saddle-like seats. The vessel roared off into the night, treating them to arguably the scariest ride he'd ever had, slapping over the waves at close to sixty knots. Who'd have guessed he'd end this whole fiasco by being rescued by a team of snake ladies and the navy SEALs?

After an hour or so on the water, they passed a major navy facility. He guessed it was Whidbey Island. The boat proceeded to a dark, silent dock and they were hustled inside a nondescript-looking building. Once inside, they took an elevator down deep inside the rocky shore. They walked interminably through an underground tunnel. Nearly a half hour later, they emerged above ground again and were transferred under umbrellas onto a P-3, a navy cargo airplane. They took off into the rain and dark, destination unknown.

And all the while, Misty said nothing to him. Everyone was quiet for the most part. He gathered that while in mission mode, the Medusas and company didn't generally speak unless necessary. Still, her silence worried him.

Vanessa Blake was miserably airsick and the team did break silence long enough to rib her about whether she was airsick or nauseous from other causes, which made both her and Jack blush. But fairly quickly after takeoff, most of the team settled down to get some rest.

He slept directly on the cold, uncomfortable floor of the plane with a rib from the plane's side digging into his back. When he woke up, the sun was shining through the single round porthole near the front of the cargo compartment. And still they flew. A couple of hours later, the plane commenced banking sharply and the engines cycled up and down several times before settling into a steady rhythm again. The ride was turbulent for a good fifteen minutes.

"We're air refueling," Misty murmured.

Where in the world were they taking him? They'd been airborne nearly eight hours according to his watch and they'd just picked up another load of fuel? They flew for several more hours before a reduction in noise from the engines and popping in his ears announced that they'd begun a descent.

They landed about a half hour later. A crew member opened the crew hatch up front, and Greg stepped outside into blinding sunlight. Rocky mountains rose to one side of the runway. A few palm trees blew in the warm breeze, and a grove of small, gnarled, ancient-looking trees grew right up to the edge of the airstrip.

He glanced over at Misty. "Olive trees? The Mediterranean?"

She nodded. "Welcome to Avgenados."

"Greece?" he asked incredulously.

"It's a private island owned by Uncle Sam."

He grinned at her. "Of course. Where else would the Medusas go to hang out after a mission besides Greece?"

She smiled back. It was the first sign of forgiveness she'd given him since he'd confessed to calling the Spetznatz team. Hope soared in his chest. He'd do whatever it took—*whatever it took*—to win her back. Who'd have guessed when he'd fled Russia, looking not to die, that he would come to America and find his reason to live?

Somewhere along the way he'd shed his cynicism. Lost his weary acceptance of the spy game as the only way he'd ever live. He'd found passion again. Passion for life and passion for love. Misty had given all that to him. She'd breezed into his life, all flirtatious wit and casual "I can handle anything" aplomb and he'd suddenly seen possibilities he'd never even imagined.

It was *she* who'd truly set him free.

A pair of Land Rovers were parked in a shack located beyond the olive grove and back from the runway a quarter mile or so. He and the others piled in and drove along a narrow, rocky, dirt road for several miles, up the side of the mountain he'd spied from the runway. As they climbed out of the vehicles at the summit, he surveyed the island at his feet. It wasn't large. Mostly rocks and olive groves. A few white stucco cottages dotted the beach far below, near a lone dock. The house at his back looked to be the only major dwelling on this side of the island.

"Is there anything on the other side of the mountain?"

Misty answered. "Nope. Just a wildlife preserve for seabirds and a lot of rocks."

"It's beautiful," he commented. "Lonely, though."

She nodded solemnly. "Not the sort of place anyone would look for a dead man."

He glanced over at her, startled. "Now what do I do? I've never been dead before."

"Now we debrief you. The others still need to hear why you called in the Spetznatz team. And then I suppose you've got a decision to make."

He looked at her sharply. "What decision?"

"Once you finish your debrief, I expect you won't be a prisoner. If you want to return to Russia, you can. Or you can stay dead, of course."

His heart dropped like a rock. She hadn't meant a decision regarding them. He'd hoped…

…But no. He'd destroyed her trust when he'd called the Russians.

In short order, the team was installed at the dining-room

table, a long wooden affair that looked about as old as the Acropolis. He looked around at the group. Decent, honorable people, one and all. They'd all been willing to put their necks on the line to save him. And to most of them, he was a complete stranger. But on the word of a person they did trust—Misty—they'd been willing to die. What he wouldn't give to have that loyal a family around him! For a family this truly was. No wonder Misty was so unswervingly loyal to them.

Of course, he could be part of this family if he wished. Misty had offered that to him, too. Except at the time he hadn't understood what it truly meant to choose sides. He'd had no idea this was waiting on her side of the fence.

Was it too late now?

By not trusting them earlier, by not explaining himself to them all, had he blown it completely?

Only one way to find out.

He spent the next several hours recounting his entire story from the moment the real Vasily Nemorov was murdered while handcuffed to his wrist until the present. Misty filled in details here and there, but he did most of the talking.

And then he was done, his story told, for better or worse. They took a break while General Wittenauer excused himself to make a call to the United States. Greg allowed himself a glance over at Misty, who gazed back at him somberly, her thoughts a mystery. If only she'd give him something, a smile or a frown, any hint as to what she was thinking or feeling. But she was inscrutable.

He excused himself from the table and stepped outside. He stared unseeingly at the turquoise and emerald and cobalt sea below. *I've blown it. I've lost the only woman I've ever loved.*

* * *

Misty felt as if she'd been holding her breath for the past three hours by the time they all finally sat down at the table again. The general had been on the phone a long time. Long enough for Dex and Isabelle to whip up sandwiches for the gang and for everyone to eat them while they waited.

Greg's debriefing had been nothing short of torture for her. To sit there quietly and not jump in to defend Greg time and again as he told his story had been almost more than she could manage.

To his credit, he left nothing out and was brutally honest in describing his actions and thought processes over the past five years. He freely admitted to working for both governments and went into as much detail as Wittenauer wanted any time the general asked for a clarification or expansion upon something Greg had said.

As confessions went, it had been a whopper.

The general spoke from the head of the table. "I've just gotten off the horn with the Director of the CIA. Further investigation has revealed that the agent Misty shot was probably on the payroll of the Russian government. A search of his home revealed an account book for an offshore checking account with inexplicable funds in it.

"The dead agent's partner is being interrogated as we speak, but has already admitted to sanitizing the scene of the Anchorage shooting. He apparently recovered several bullets from the scene and escorted a woman away from the crime scene by offering her a ride home. The Director has sent a team to pick up the woman for questioning, but he expects she's the witness from inside the store whose life Greg saved."

Wittenauer looked down the table at her. "The Director

expects that after he receives her deposition, all charges against you will be dropped, Sidewinder. It was a clear case of self-defense. And even if it wasn't, the evidence has been tampered with so badly, the CIA could never make any charges stick."

Misty exhaled slowly. "That's good news," she said quietly. She looked down the table at Greg. He was smiling jubilantly. Okay, so it was great news, and she was pretty darned relieved. She allowed herself to match his smile. Their gazes met warmly for an unguarded moment, then slid away from each other awkwardly.

"So, Greg," General Wittenauer continued. "The next step's up to you. What do you want to do?"

Misty's gaze snapped to Greg. She was startled to see him looking steadily back at her. Then he said evenly, "There's one question you haven't asked me yet, general."

"What's that?"

"What I plan to do with my database of juicy files. After all, you could always just take it from me."

Wittenauer looked at him expectantly. Brute force wasn't Wittenauer's style. He was much more inclined to pleasantly hand a person a piece of rope and let them hang themselves with it.

It all came down to this. What *would* Greg do when the chips were down? Misty's breath caught in her throat. Was he about to offer the files for sale to the United States or not? Hope and dread fluttered in her chest.

Greg spoke slowly. "I've learned in the past week that what matters to me isn't money or power or being a hero. I want out of the game for good. I want to grow old in peace. And I don't want to spend the rest of my life alone."

Her teammates' glances swiveled toward her, but she ignored them all, her own gaze riveted on Greg.

He continued, choosing his words carefully. "The Russian government believes that Vasily Nemorov is dead. And so he is. Let's keep it that way. I'm done with that part of my life."

"And Greg Mitchell?" Wittenauer asked.

"He died in an explosion in upstate Washington. But as his final act, he left something for his employer. A parting gift, if you will."

Greg reached into his pants pocket and pulled out a small, square object about the length of his thumb on each side. He laid it on the table before the general. "It's all there. Everything. Every last file I collected in Moscow. Dirt on world leaders and prominent businessmen, identities of Russian mafia figures, lists of Russian spies in the United States, secret deals Russia has made with its allies—and enemies—assessments of Russian nuclear strength, you name it. Everything that came across my desk that I thought might be remotely useful to the United States."

Misty blinked. What he described was a treasure trove for the American intelligence community. It could take the Americans months or even years to sort through everything he'd brought them. And he was *giving* it to them?

She burst out, "What happened to selling it to the highest bidder?"

He glanced down the table at her, then back at the general. "Would you mind if Sidewinder and I had a private conversation outside?"

"Be my guest."

Damned if that wasn't a smile hovering around the corners of Wittenauer's mouth. Misty scowled at her boss on the way past him and muttered, "Don't say anything. Not a word."

She stepped out onto the tiled verandah. The sun was setting in the west, sending a brilliant column of red across the calm ocean below. Greg said nothing. He merely studied her in silence. He was so achingly handsome in that contemplative moment it almost hurt to look at him.

Finally, she asked cautiously, "What did you want to talk about?"

He smiled gently. "I think you know."

She frowned. "I want to hear you say it."

"All right. I want to talk about us."

"What about us?"

"Is there an us?"

She risked looking up at him. "Did you mean what you said in there?"

"I gave up my one ace-in-the-hole, Misty. I handed over everything to Wittenauer. My financial windfall, my personal security, my future safety. All of it."

"Why?"

"You have to ask? I did it for you. Don't you see? I jumped off the fence."

Something cracked in her chest. Her heart felt as if it was breaking open.

He continued, "I choose America. I choose *you*. Not your face. Your soul. The woman beneath."

She shattered into a million pieces right then and there. With a sob, she flung herself into his arms. "Are you sure?" she choked out.

He laughed. "Ahh, *milochka*, I've never been more sure of anything in my life."

And in a single sentence, he'd made her whole again. All of her. For the first time in her adult life, she was at peace with herself from the inside out.

"Will you have me, Misty? In unflinching honesty an

wild passion and all the tenderness I can show you for the rest of our lives?"

She smiled brilliantly. "How can a girl say no to that?"

He wrapped her in his arms and they embraced for a long time, their arms wrapped around each other and his heart thudding steadily beneath her ear. Quiet settled around them. The sun set at their feet and in that moment all the world was at peace. And the future stretched before them, fresh and new, waiting for them to write the next chapters of their lives. Together.

* * * * *

Welcome to cowboy country...

Turn the page for a sneak preview of
TEXAS BABY
by
Kathleen O'Brien
An exciting new title from Harlequin Superromance
for everyone who loves stories about the West.

Harlequin Superromance—
Where life and love weave together in emotional and
unforgettable ways.

CHAPTER ONE

CHASE TRANSFERRED his gaze to the road and identified a foreign spot on the horizon. A car. Almost half a mile away, where the straight, tree-lined drive met the public road. He could tell it was coming too fast, but judging the speed of a vehicle moving straight toward you was tricky.

It wasn't until it was about two hundred yards away that he realized the driver must be drunk…or crazy. Or both.

The guy was going maybe sixty. On a private drive, out here in ranch country, where kids or horses or tractors or stupid chickens might come darting out any minute—that was criminal. Chase straightened from his comfortable slouch and waved his hands.

"Slow down, you fool," he called out. He took the porch steps quickly and began walking fast down the driveway.

The car veered oddly, from one lane to another, then up onto the slight rise of the thick green spring grass. It just barely missed the fence.

"Slow down, damn it!"

He couldn't see the driver, and he didn't recognize this automobile. It was small and old, and couldn't have cost much even when it was new. It was probably white, but now it needed either a wash or a new paint job or both.

"Damn it, what's wrong with you?"

At the last minute, he had to jump away, because the idiot behind the wheel clearly wasn't going to turn to avoid a collision. He couldn't believe it. The car kept coming, finally slowing a little, but it was too late.

Still going about thirty miles an hour, it slammed into the large, white-brick pillar that marked the front boundaries of the house. The pillar wasn't going to give an inch, so the car had to. The front end folded up like a paper fan.

It seemed to take forever for the car to settle, as if the trauma happened in slow motion, reverberating from the front to the back of the car in ripples of destruction. The front windshield suddenly seemed to ice over with lethal bits of glassy frost. Then the side windows exploded.

The front driver's door wrenched open, as if the car wanted to expel its contents. Metal buckled hideously. Small pieces, like hubcaps and mirrors, skipped and ricocheted insanely across the oyster-shell driveway.

Finally, everything was still. Into the silence, a plume of steam shot up like a geyser, smelling of rust and heat. Its snake-like hiss almost smothered the low, agonized moan of the driver.

Chase's anger had disappeared. He didn't feel anything but a dull sense of disbelief. Things like this didn't happen in real life. Not in his life. Maybe the sun had actually put him to sleep....

But he was already kneeling beside the car. The driver was a woman. The frosty glass-ice of the windshield was dotted with small flecks of blood. She must have hit it with her head, because just below her hairline a red liquid was seeping out. He touched it. He tried to wipe it away before it reached her eyebrow, though, of course that made no sense at all. Her eyes were shut.

Was she conscious? Did he dare move her? Her dress was covered in glass, and the metal of the car was sticking out lethally in all the wrong places.

Then he remembered, with an intense relief, that every good medical man in the county was here, just behind the house, drinking his champagne. He found his phone and paged Trent.

The woman moaned again.

Alive, then. Thank God for that.

He saw Trent coming toward him, starting out at a lope, but quickly switching to a full run.

"Get Dr. Marchant," Chase called. "Don't bother with 9-1-1."

Trent didn't take long to assess the situation. A fraction of a second, and he began pulling out his cell phone and running toward the house.

The yelling seemed to have roused the woman. She opened her eyes. They were blue and clouded with pain and confusion.

"Chase," she said.

His breath stalled. His head pulled back. "What?"

Her only answer was another moan, and he wondered if he had imagined the word. He reached around her and put his arm behind her shoulders. She was tiny. Probably petite by nature, but surely way too thin. He could feel her shoulder blades pushing against her skin, as fragile as the wishbone in a turkey.

She seemed to have passed out, so he put his other arm

under her knees and lifted her out. He tried to avoid the jagged metal, but her skirt caught on a piece and the tearing sound seemed to wake her again.

"No," she said. "Please."

"I'm just trying to help," he said. "It's going to be all right."

She seemed profoundly distressed. She wriggled in his arms, and she was so weak, like a broken bird. It made him feel too big and brutish. And intrusive. As if touching her this way, his bare hands against the warm skin behind her knees, were somehow a transgression.

He wished he could be more delicate. But he smelled gasoline, and he knew it wasn't safe to leave her here.

Finally he heard the sound of voices, as guests began to run around the side of the house, alerted by Trent. Dr. Marchant was at the front, racing toward them as if he were forty instead of seventy. Susannah was right behind him, her green dress floating around her trim legs.

"Please," the woman in his arms murmured again. She looked at him, the expression in her blue eyes lost and bewildered. He wondered if she might be on drugs. Hitting her head on the windshield might account for this unfocused, glazed look, but it couldn't explain the crazy driving.

"Please, put me down. Susannah… The wedding…"

Chase's arms tightened instinctively, and he froze in his tracks. She whimpered, and he realized he might be hurting her. "Say that again?"

"The wedding. I have to stop it."

* * * * *

Be sure to look for TEXAS BABY,
available September 11, 2007,
as well as other fantastic Superromance titles
available in September.

ATHENA FORCE

Heart-pounding romance and thrilling adventure.

Professional negotiator Lindsey Novak is faced with her biggest challenge—to buy back Teal Arnett, a young woman with unique powers. In the process Lindsey uncovers a devastating plot that involves scientists from around the globe, and all of them lead to one woman who is bent on destroying Athena Academy...at any cost.

LOOK FOR

THE GOOD THIEF

by Judith Leon

Available September wherever you buy books.

REQUEST YOUR FREE BOOKS!

2 FREE NOVELS PLUS 2 FREE GIFTS!

Silhouette® Romantic

SUSPENSE

Sparked by Danger, Fueled by Passion!

COMING NEXT MONTH

#1479 MIRANDA'S REVENGE—Ruth Wind
Sisters of the Mountain
With the clock ticking and a murder trial on the horizon,
Miranda Rousseau has one last chance at clearing her sister's name.
But James Marquez, the tall, sexy private investigator she's hired to
solve the case, is fast becoming much more than just a colleague in
the face of danger.

#1480 TOP-SECRET BRIDE—Nina Bruhns
Mission: Impassioned
Two spies pose as husband and wife in order to uncover a potential mole
in their corporations. As they work together, each new piece of the puzzle
pulls them further into danger, and into each other's arms....

#1481 SHADOW WHISPERS—Linda Conrad
Night Guardians
She is determined to have her revenge on the Skinwalker cult. He's seeking
the truth about his family. Now they will join forces to uncover secrets long
buried…and discover a passion that could threaten their lives.

#1482 SINS OF THE STORM—Jenna Mills
Midnight Secrets
After years in hiding, Camille Fontenot returns home to solve the
mystery of her father's death. But someone doesn't want Camille
to succeed, and she must turn to an old flame for protection…while
fighting an all-consuming desire.

SRSCNM0807